CALHOON

CALHOON

Thorne Douglas

A FAWCETT GOLD MEDAL BOOK
Fawcett Books, Greenwich, Connecticut

CALHOON

All characters in this book are fictional, and any resemblance to persons living or dead is purely coincidental.

Chapter 1

Getting off the steamer at Powderhorn, he bought a horse in Indianola with the last of his money: a good Morgan sold cheap for gold. Carefully, patiently, he made inquiries, but no one had heard of the man he sought. So many people who had left Texas before the war had come back, so many who had fought for it had not; there were Yankee soldiers now and strangers like himself pouring in from every quarter of the compass; the whole state was in turmoil, and guerrilla bands still roamed, and outlaws. There were not enough soldiers to put them down, and anyhow, all the soldiers were out on the frontier on guard against Comanches. Everything was in confusion and nobody knew anything except that they had been beaten, the slaves were supposed to be free, and Confederate money and Confederate bonds were worthless. Then he caught a breath of rumor, a name and a town, the two linked. The town was Double Oaks, on the south side of the Nueces and farther west. He rode that way, living off the land, knowing that the inhabitants of the sparsely settled country had little enough to share with unexpected strangers. Anyhow, there were plenty of deer, and he was a good shot.

In Texas not much more than a week, he was impressed. The wild tales he'd heard from Hood's cavalrymen were not so wild after all. Piney woods, good black farmland, great ranges of high grass—he had seen them all. Now he was south of the river and in the brush country, and in some ways it was the most spectacular of all. The dusty little wagon track he followed was hemmed in on both sides with great thickets of the stuff: mesquite, cactus, yucca, a stunted kind of oak, and a hundred other plants whose names he did not know; and most were equipped with thorns. Each side of the track was laced together in walls that looked impenetrable, but he had spent too much time hunting in the swamps at home—and fighting in them, too—to think they really were. In such places there were always game and cattle paths. Here, especially, the paths of cattle.

Because the brush was full of them, thousands, hundreds of thousands of skinny, longhorned brutes of an unthrifty-looking breed; they infested it like fleas in a stray dog's shaggy fur. Only rarely did he see them—they were as wild and shy as deer—but occasionally a few of them would break across the road, running with unbelievable swiftness for bovine creatures. And at night, when he camped deep in the brush—well off the road, taking to heart the stories of roving bands of men who would kill a stranger for his horse and gun—he could hear the long-horns all around him. They crackled and rustled on every side, and the cows bellowed, and the calves blatted, and the bulls rumbled and grunted constantly. He wondered how their owners—if they had any—were ever going to dig them out of this jungle. And if they did, where they would sell them in a South that had no money left to pay for beef. They occupied only a small part of his thoughts, though; mostly he lived in the past, racked by grief and loss and bitterness. When it became more than he could bear, he would summon up the hatred, and that would pull him into the future and help somewhat.

When he rode on during the day, all he thought about was the road; he stayed continually alert, his senses tuned and keen, his left hand balancing the Henry rifle across his saddle pommel, fully loaded and ready for instant use. After all the years of combat that had become habit with him; that was why, on this hot, drowsy afternoon, when he was still ten miles east of Double Oaks, he heard the men from a long way off and reined in the Morgan, frowning.

Calhoon was in his late twenties. Dismounted, he would have stood well over six feet. His shoulders were very broad, but he was so gaunted with travel and short rations

that his dirty, sweat-soaked broadcloth shirt hung around
his torso like a bag. His face was weathered and deeply
burned, his cheekbones high and prominent, his nose big
and straight, his mouth wide and thin over a buttress of a
chin. Beneath black brows his eyes were the gray of gun-
metal. His hat was gray, too, a Confederate officer's with
the insigne removed; his pants matched it, and he wore
high black boots. In addition to the Henry he carried a
Colt .36 Navy revolver in a holster on his left hip and a
knife with a double-edged blade, the kind called an Arkansas toothpick, in a sheath built for it in his left boot.
He held the rifle always with his left hand and the reins,
too; for he had no right one. Where that should have been,
the wrist ended in a stump encased in a wrapping of heavy
leather.

Keeping the Morgan tight-gathered, he listened. The
voices came from around a sharp bend in the trail a few
hundred yards away, and there was both anger and mock-
ery in them, although he could not discern the words. Calhoon considered. They could be honest cowhunters, trav-
elers like himself, guerrillas, or road agents. He looked at
the brush on either side and ahead and found that this
stretch of it was even more tightly laced than usual; he
could see no path through it. So, whatever they were, if he
were to make Double Oaks by dark, he'd have to pass by
or through them; there was no way to go around.

Of course, he told himself, he could drop back a mile,
find a trail into the brush, pull off there, wait a while, then
ride on. It was what any sensible man would do. The trouble was, he had not felt sensible, not since he had heard
that name linked with Double Oaks. The closer he got to
that town, the greater the impatience rising in him and the
hatred. And now, just as he was about to reach the goal he
had pursued for so long, he was interrupted, balked.

He was past letting anybody do that to him now, this
late in the game, so he made what he knew was an irration-
al and dangerous decision. He put the Morgan forward in
an easy walk, a gait at which its hoofs made no sound in
the soft dust, and he raised the Henry. Going forward
slowly, he could presently make out voices and words.

There were, he judged, at least four men around the bend; and presently one sentence came clear. "Awright, Ed," somebody ordered, the voice thick, slurred, drunken. "Drop the loop around his goddamn neck and less git it over with."

That was when Calhoon put the horse into a faster, gathered walk. He rounded the turn, and then he reined it in hard. There on his right the brush opened out into a grassy clearing, dominated by a great live oak in its center. On one side of the clearing a buckskin horse stood tethered, head down. In the shade of the oak four riders sat their mounts. Calhoon's view was blocked by the horses; he squinted. A man stood in the center of the circle, his hands held awkwardly in front of him—tied, probably. One of the riders grasped a rawhide loop; the end was around the neck of the standing man, Calhoon thought. The rope ran over a big live oak limb to a saddle horn. The man in that saddle had his spurs cocked, ready to ram them home.

It was a hanging he had come upon; its victim seemed to be short, perhaps stocky. The mounted men were all looking at the victim and were unaware of Calhoon's presence. Dressed in narrow-brimmed hats with chin straps, leather jackets, and leather pants over denims, all armed with holstered pistols, they sat on their mounts, grinning at the man and passing around a nearly empty bottle.

Once more Calhoon had to make a decision. It was a hard one, but he made it; and then he rode into the clearing. A man with a bush of curly red beard took a swig from the bottle and said, "Well, 'Lias, you sure you ain't gonna beg?"

Contemptuously the bound man snorted.

Redbeard's voice turned hard. "Hell, Ed, take him up."

"Sho," said the man with the rope tied to his saddle horn. He was about to ram home the spurs when Calhoon said, in a voice that carried, "Gentlemen, stand fast."

For perhaps two seconds the clearing was absolutely silent as the four riders swung their horses, staring at Calhoon and the Henry. The man on the ground moved, too. "Mister—" he said hoarsely.

Then the man with the red beard—left hand clutching the bottle, blue eyes fixed on the muzzle of the Henry, right hand poised near his waist, not far from the holstered Army Colt—put his horse forward a pace. "All right, stranger," he rasped, eyes raking over the gray hat, the gray trousers. "What the hell is this?"

"I was about to ask you the same question," Calhoon said. He sat the Morgan outwardly relaxed; inwardly, his stomach was tight clenched, and he felt sweat running down his flanks. As the circle had parted, Calhoon had realized the man was black. Damnit, he thought, if I had only known he was black. . . . But Calhoon was in too deep to get out now.

"You can see what it is," Redbeard said. "We're about to hang a nigger." His voice had a flat, un-Southern twang. "Judgin' from the color of your hat and pants, that shouldn't upset you too bad. Put down that rifle and ride on."

"Maybe in a minute," Calhoon said.

"No maybe to it, less you want to get crosswise of Tod Isaacs and his Regulators."

"You Isaacs?"

"I am that gentleman. And these are just a small party of my men. Plenty more where they come from." Above his beard his cheeks were purplish with broken veins, his nose ended in a red bulb. But there was keenness and intelligence in his eyes. "So if you place any value on your health, you'll take to the road again."

"Like I said, in a minute. What's this buck done?"

"Why," Isaacs said, "he stole a horse belongin' to me. That one over there." He waved the bottle at the buckskin.

"That's a lie!" the black man roared. "That buckskin I raised from a foal! He a good brush horse, and when I wouldn't sell it to this trash, they bushwhacked me out heah on this road!" His eyes glittered, his skin shone with sweat, but there was no fear in him at all as he looked at Calhoon. "I kin prove that horse doesn't belong to this trash, you ask Henry Gannon—"

"Trash," Calhoon said. "That's bad language for a man with a rope around his neck."

"Trash's trash," the black said. "Rope don't change what trash is."

"You are plumb uppity, aren't you?" Calhoon asked.

"I'm a free man. I won't crawl to nobody."

Isaacs said easily, "You see, Reb? He's got a bad mouth, no respect for anybody. Now why don't you ride on and let us give him what he's got comin', Mr. . . ."

"Calhoon. Lucius Calhoon from Clarendon County, South Carolina."

The man with the rope around his saddle horn laughed. "South Ca'lina, eh?" He had a very long neck and a very small head atop it, which kept twisting restlessly like a nervous snake. His cheeks were furred with two days' brindle beard. "Yeah, you talk like one of them planters. Reckon you used to own niggers yourself. Bet you hung many a buck to teach him a lesson."

Calhoon said, "I used to own two hundred. They all died natural deaths, those that died. I've ordered lashes on occasion, but I've never hanged one." His eyes shuttled back to Isaacs. He had these men sized up now, and he liked nothing about them. He had seen their kind in both armies, and in his time he had disciplined his share for offenses against civilians: looting, murder, rape . . . His voice instinctively fell into a tone of harsh command. "Isaacs, what proof you got that horse was yours but stolen?"

"Proof? South Ca'lina, you talk foolishness. I *say* he did. Around here no more proof's needed. I'da brought 'im up in front of Weymouth, only then the Army woulda interfered—"

That was when Calhoon sat up straight, his heart beating faster. Now his stomach unclenched, and the sweat stopped flowing, and something began to sing in him. "Weymouth?"

"County judge in Double Oaks. Also chief Treasury agent for this district."

Calhoon let out a long breath. "That would be Gordon Weymouth from Victoria."

"No. Josh, his old man." Isaacs jerked his head impatiently. "Friend, ride on unless—"

"Take the rope off him," Calhoon said.

"Whut?" Isaacs blinked.

"I said, take the rope off his neck. Cut his bonds. You there with that tie around your saddle horn. You move that horse, I'll blow you out of the saddle."

"Now wait just a damn minute," Isaacs rasped, eyes slits now. He held the bottle far out to the left, his right hand spreading.

"You're a friend of Weymouth's?"

"You better damn well know it. And if you—"

"Take off that rope. Now!" Calhoon snapped the words.

Isaacs sat very still for perhaps a second. Then his mouth, inside his shag of red beard, curled. "One against four, and that one with a single hand. Reb, you are too big for those gray britches—" That was when he started to reach for his gun.

Calhoon fired the Henry. Its sound was thunderous in the clearing's drowsy silence. The bottle in Isaac's left hand exploded into fragments, and his horse shied and bucked, stung by glass. In the same second, the movement so swift it was a blur, Calhoon had the rifle stock clamped under his left arm, his right forearm beneath the balance, and with his left hand he worked the lever. Then the gun was centered again squarely on Isaac's chest, as the red-bearded man got his horse reined in. The others gawked, frozen in astonishment at the speed of it all.

"Now," Lucius Calhoon said, his voice very even, yet a little breathless with a kind of killer eagerness, "if you want to live a minute longer, you do this. You take that gun out of your holster easy with your left hand and drop it on the green. Then you swing over there and cut that rope and get his hands loose. Without any tricks. Otherwise, your Regulators'll be huntin' for a new Isaacs."

Isaacs' nose stood out like a flare against the paleness of his face. He looked into Calhoon's eyes. Then, very cautiously he said, "The rest of you stand hitched." He reached across his body, drew his big Army Colt, and let it drop. His eyes were blue flames. But he spoke no word as he wheeled his horse, pulled a knife from its sheath, bent, cut the rawhide rope above the black man's neck, then sawed through the bonds.

Calhoon's gaze shuttled back and forth from Isaacs to Ed to the other two, both younger and, in this leaderless moment, paralyzed. But he kept the rifle trained on Isaacs.

When the black man was free, Calhoon said, "Now throw that knife over in the brush."

Isaacs did. The man called Ed made a strangled sound in his throat. "Some Reb. Where'd you steal that gray hat?"

Calhoon said harshly, "Let's say I traded three years of war, a year in prison, a plantation, and a hand for it. Get down off your horse. You too, Isaacs, and the others. Dismount and walk over to that tree carefully, hands high. First man breaks gets a bullet from the Henry. Then I unlimber the Colt, and I'm even faster and better with it."

For one rebellious second the four of them were poised. They knew, and Calhoon knew, that he could not take them all, that they could kill him. But they had seen enough, too, to know that one or two of them would die in the effort, and they were not the kind of men to push such a matter to that length. They wanted the odds where they had been before he arrived: all on their side. Calhoon, meanwhile, dominated them with the rifle barrel and his eyes, his presence, as he had dealt with rebellious troops before. The second stretched, and then they broke; and Ed swung down. After a pause Isaacs followed suit, and then the other two did also, hands going up.

"To the tree," Calhoon reiterated.

Holding their hands high, they walked to the trunk of the enormous live oak. The black man stood there with a broad grin on his face.

"You," Calhoon said, "boy—"

The grin vanished. "My name Elias Whitton."

"Get their guns. Throw 'em over in the brush, deep. Take those rifles off their saddles, too. Then mount your horse, gather up their horses. Don't make a break or I'll kill you."

"You'll—"

"You heard me," Calhoon said harshly. "Do what I said." He added, "And don't block my line of fire."

He watched narrowly as the black man complied, going to the men, whisking their guns from holsters, tossing them into the thickets. The way Whitton never blocked the muzzle of the Henry told him that he had experience as a fighting man. Then Whitton took the carbines from their saddle rings, threw them after the pistols. He gathered up the reins of the four horses, led them to the buckskin—it was small, scarred, with strange knots and it certainly did not, to Calhoon, look worth a hanging—and swung up as lithely as a cat.

"Take those horses out on the road. Wait there," Calhoon said.

Whitton clucked, the buckskin moved, and the horses followed.

Calhoon spurred the Morgan forward. Isaacs' eyes blazed up at him. "If you have a complaint to make against this man about that horse, I'll have him in Double Oaks, waiting for you. I'll be there myself. If you don't show up by noon tomorrow, he goes free. Your horses— I'll leave 'em three miles down the road. You'll find 'em hitched somewhere in the open. You got further business with me, I'll be in Double Oaks."

"We got business with you," Isaacs said hoarsely.

"All right," said Calhoon. "Until later then." He swung the Morgan, spurred it. In the road the black man waited with the other horses. "Ride!" Calhoon snapped.

"Yaah!" Whitton yelled. There was the thunder of hoofs as the buckskin broke into a flashing run, followed by the riderless mounts. Calhoon spurred the Morgan hard and sent it pounding after.

For three miles they stretched their mounts along that narrow aisle through the thickets. Then Calhoon yelled, "Pull up!"

Ahead, Elias paid no attention. Bent low in the saddle, he lashed the bucksin with the rein ends. Calhoon swore and lined the Henry. He fired it, clamped its stock, reloaded, all in a flash. The lead whined deliberately high just over Whitton's ear. The black man yanked the buckskin to a sliding halt, and it was almost knocked over as the other horses nearly plowed into it. Then Whitton whirled his mount.

Calhoon centered the Henry on his chest. "Damnit, didn't you hear me tell you to halt?"

Whitton stared back at him without expression. Calhoon saw how wholly black his skin was, how flat the nose and thick the lips, how the dark eyes blazed beneath crags of brows. Gaboon or Middle Congo blood, he thought instinctively, with the expertise of a man brought up to judge the blood of blacks like the blood of cattle or horses. A stubborn breed that this man sprang from, wild, savage, intractable . . . Whitton's voice was deep. "Let them bastards walk to Double Oaks. All the way."

"No. I said I'd leave the horses here. I keep my promises. All of them. Including the one about taking you into town. You're my prisoner and don't you forget that. Now dismount and tie those animals."

Whitton stared at him a moment longer, then swung down, tethered the led horses. In a flashing instant he was back in the buckskin's saddle and had reined the small, wiry mount around to face Calhoon.

"Mister," he said, "we ain't goin' into Double Oaks."

"I think we are," Calhoon said, keeping the Henry centered.

"No. We goin' through the brush." Whitton drew in a deep breath that made his barrel chest swell. "You got to understand. I ain't scared of Weymouth. Weymouth can't touch me; I go direct to Captain Killraine. He protect me. Because I black. But you white, you are Reb, and Killraine don't protect no Rebs. You go into Double Oaks, it'll be Weymouth from one side, Isaacs from the other, you be a dead man by mornin'. Isaacs talked true, he got a lot more riders, and they all in Double Oaks right now. Bad men, worst scum you ever seen. Trash, like I said. Didn't fight on neither side in the war, bushwhacked wherever they could make some money. But Weymouth, he got use for 'em now." He hesitated. "I reckon I owe you some thanks. So you follow me, I take you to a place they don't know where you can hide. Cover your tracks, come daylight, you can ride out wide around Double Oaks and be gone."

"That's kind of you," Calhoon said. "But no thanks. Maybe I've got some business there with Weymouth. Anyhow, I'm going in, and you go along as prisoner."

Whitton let out a gusty breath. "Look, white man. You save my skin, I'm tryin' to save yours. I don't like bein' beholden to anybody. Now I got to take that artillery away from you to make you do right for your own good?"

Calhoon stiffened. "You try it, boy."

"I told you, my name is—" He never finished the sentence but spurred the buckskin, and the horse leaped forward with amazing speed. At the same time Whitton dropped under its neck, clinging by one foot over the saddle in a way that Calhoon had never seen done before. He fired the Henry, but the shot went wild, and then as he clamped it under his arm, the buckskin had slammed into his mustang, and Whitton was upright again, had grabbed the rifle, and wrenched it from Calhoon's grasp before Calhoon could get another round in.

The rifle went flying; Whitton made a grab for the Colt. At that instant Calhoon swung his right arm. It came across his body, and the leather-bound stump where the hand should have been slammed into Whitton's temple. It made a sodden sound as it connected, and as Whitton's buckskin veered, the black man fell limply from the saddle, landing on his back. Calhoon's left hand swooped down, brought out the Colt. When Whitton opened his eyes and stared up at him, the .36's muzzle was aimed straight at him.

"On your horse," Calhoon said harshly. He jerked the right, handless forearm. "There's a pound of buckshot," he said, "inside that leather wrapping."

Something stirred in Whitton's eyes as he got slowly to his feet. "Man, for an hombre with one hand you got it all worked out, ain't you?"

"A man with one hand has got to work it all out," Calhoon said.

With almost delicate wariness now Whitton mounted the buckskin. Calhoon never took either eyes or gun off him until he had the Morgan in position. Then, out of necessity he had to bend far down, swiftly grab the fallen Henry by the barrel, jerk it up. He came up in a blur, gun still trained on Whitton, but the man had not moved.

Calhoon, pulling the Henry by the barrel and aiming the Colt, managed to get the rifle across his saddle. "Now," he said. "Into Double Oaks."

"Awright," said Whitton. "You can put that gun away. I won't break again."

"You do," Calhoon said, "you're dead."

"No. You go to Double Oaks, you are. But—" he shrugged. "It your funeral."

Calhoon said, "That remains to be seen. Now turn your horse and ride."

Chapter 2

The narrow road wound through the brush like a snake with a broken back, and they went in single file at a high lope, Elias Whitton in the forefront, Calhoon behind, the Henry scabbarded now and the Colt in its holster. Calhoon stared at the great, broad back of the black man on the buckskin, keeping the Morgan closed up tight, and thought: another one. Another one to sucker me into trouble, into a fight I didn't want . . .

And yet there was no regret in him. As tired as he was of blacks, as much as he hated the very sight of their dark faces when he thought of all they had cost him, he knew himself too well to think that he could have sat idly by or ridden unquestioningly on while four men lynched a man, white or black. But there was something else, too. Weymouth. Isaacs had threatened him with that name. Josh Weymouth, not Gordon. The father, not the son. But father or son, right now it made no difference, he was on the right track; he was closing in. If the younger Weymouth was not in Double Oaks, the older one would know where he was. Calhoon took his eyes off of Whitton long enough to look down at his right forearm. He thought again of the punishment cell at Belle Isle, of himself stripped naked, the ropes tight around his wrist, his body stretched so that only his toes touched the ground . . . He had killed so damned many men in combat that by the time he'd been captured, he was relieved to become a prisoner, glad to be rid of the necessity for any more senseless killing. He had never dreamed then that the day would come when he would hunger for the death of another man with an appetite stronger than that for food, drink, or even women . . .

Then Whitton brought the buckskin to a rearing halt,

17

and Calhoon almost collided with him. He dropped his hand to his Colt.

Whitton turned in the saddle. "Nemmind that. You won't take me with that buckshot a second time, but I ain't comin' after you. Listen. There's riders up ahead." His voice was low, almost a whisper. "I don't know who . . . But it could easy be more of Isaacs' men, them Regulators."

Calhoon motioned him to silence, reined the Morgan past the buckskin. He heard it then, the distant drum of hoofs, four or five men coming hard.

"If they Isaacs' people, we in a squeeze," Whitton said. "A bunch behind, a bunch ahead. You may be good, but you ain't that good."

"Might be soldiers, maybe cowmen . . ."

"And a fifty percent chance they ain't, or better. You so damned determined to git to Double Oaks you want to fight your way through? Or you want to follow me into the brush?"

Calhoon hesitated, biting his lip. Whitton was making sense. "All right," he said. "The brush." His eyes scanned the low, thickety walls on either side. "But where? I see no trail."

"Trail?" Whitton laughed. "Man, I make a trail. You follow me." He turned the buckskin, then hesitated. "Neither you or that Morgan ever been in brush before. It gonna be rough. You both gonna lose some skin. Keep your arm up in fronta your face but don't shut your eyes when you see a limb comin'. You do that, next one's liable to knock you outa the saddle. I'll try to dodge the cholla; that's the worst. Come on." Then he spurred the buckskin straight into a clump of mesquite. It seemed to open and close around him like a cloud. Calhoon braced himself, crashed the Morgan after.

In his time he'd hunted and fought in the thickest swamps of the South, but he'd never made a ride like this. He ducked and dodged, shielding his face with his arm as Whitton had instructed. Within a dozen yards the hat was clawed from his head, and he caught it just in time. Limbs

whipped and grabbed him, lashing mercilessly, and most
of them had thorns. The Morgan snorted, flinched, as its
hide was raked by spiked foliage, but it went on gallantly.
There was nothing to do but give it its head, let it dodge
the obstacles as best it could. Once his Colt was seized,
nearly pulled from his holster; again a branch of catclaw
caught the rifle butt protruding from the scabbard. Ahead,
Whitton was a dim figure, riding hard, dodging and weav-
ing, barely visible through the foliage, and now Calhoon
saw the reason for all the leather and tough denim Texans
wore. Twenty yards, thirty, and his broadcloth shirt was
tattered, his skin raked and bleeding, his gray pants
snagged and ripped. The Morgan was taking worse punishment, plunging through prickly pear, crashing through
Spanish dagger. And yet it went on at full gallop, and
somehow, despite the agony of this ride a kind of exulta-
tion grew in Calhoon. He thought of bear hunts he had
made in the swamps and the high mountains of the
Carolinas before the war, the same kind of wild rides
through catbriar and cane in the lowgrounds, laurel and
tangled rhododendron in the hills. All the same, after
more than a half mile he knew neither he nor the Morgan
could go on this way cross-country, smashing down the
chaparral and taking such punishment. Then he quit
thinking, abandoned himself to the wild, crazy ride, doing
his best to dodge the worst of the thickets and still follow
Whitton, slipping at full tilt through them like a frightened
deer.

And then blessedly they struck a trail. The Morgan
grunted in pain as it smashed through prickly pear up to
its chest, and then they were in a low, narrow aisle the
width of a single horse. Whitton had reined in, waiting. "It
get better now," he said. "There be cow paths in here I kin
follow pretty well to where we want to go. But it still be
rough in places." He swung down. "Lemme check that
horse. He got a bad thorn in a joint, he be ruined for life."
He ran his hands over the Morgan's knees and pasterns,
then went to the hindquarters. The Morgan gathered itself to kick, then to Calhoon's surprise, stood fast under

Whitton's touch as the black man made a crooning sound. Whitton straightened up. "He all right. Follow me, we go easier now."

"Where we bound?"

"Henry Gannon's place. Not his house, though. There an ole cabin in the brush. You and me both, likely Henry, too, better spend the night there. Isaacs be mad as hell, come lookin' for me at Henry's house. Now. You got a coat?"

"Yeah." Calhoon was already untying it from behind his saddle. It was heavy wool, and the heat was stifling. He had to pick thorns from his flesh before he could put it on. Meanwhile, Whitton said, "Lemme have that slicker, too."

Calhoon handed him the stiff India rubber garment in which the coat had been rolled. Whitton shook it out, went to the Morgan, tied the sleeves around the animal's neck so that the rest of the garment hung down over its chest like a shield. "That help a little bit if they come after us and we got to run cross-country again. Cram that hat down tight on your head, take your bandanna, tie it down around your chin, that'll hold it on. Use a slip knot, a limb hook it, you kin break your neck, you ridin' at a run. You plan to stay this part of Texas, you gonna need a brush jacket and some chaps and tapaderos for them stirrups. But it be easier when you got the right outfit and you and your horse git to know the brush."

Calhoon looked around. "This stuff is hell."

"You git over close to the coast, it even worse. You ain't felt nothin' yet until you ram into a clump of ebony. And—" he pointed to a clump of tall, branched cactus— "—cholla. Stay outa that. You jest brush against it, you fulla thorns that'll leave you or your horse in powerful bad shape, especially you try to pull 'em out with main strength." He swung up into the saddle. "Now. You ready to ride?"

Calhoon listened; behind them in the brush there was a crackling. Whitton grinned. "That no rider, that a long-horn sneakin' away. Come on, let's go." And he touched the buckskin with his spurs.

Even on the cattle trail it was rough. There was more room for the horse, but mesquite in places or the feathery branches of huisache arched across to seize the rider, and Calhoon, ducking low and following Whitton at a trot, still took limb whips and thorn rakes. But he was, at this slower pace, beginning to get the feel of the brush now, and he started to move automatically in the saddle to dodge the worst of it. The coat helped, too, immensely. But in the heat within the brush it seemed to him that he was being steamed alive inside it. Sweat poured down his flanks, trickled down his forehead, nearly blinding him. He was afraid to rub his sleeve across his eyes for fear of jabbing them with a thorn the wool might have picked up. He mopped it away with his fingers and followed Whitton. The buckskin was cat-footed, shifting and dodging automatically as obstacles appeared; the Morgan learned to guide on it and began to do the same.

Occasionally they paused to rest the horses and listen for pursuit, but there was nothing behind them that Calhoon could hear. Whitton did not seem surprised. "Them Regulators of Isaacs'. They come down from Kansas and Missouri, they don't know nothin' about the chaparral. That one of the reasons Isaacs wants my horse so bad. He learned how much a good brush horse is worth in this country."

Another hour, two, of that: Whitton seemed to know every cattle path and deer trail in here, and he followed the intricate web of them with certainty. Then, ahead Calhoon saw the crowns of two big live oaks, and presently the men came out of the brush and into the clearing under them. There the crumbling ruins of an old log cabin and a few rotted outbuildings testified to the breaking of some settler's dream. Near the clearing's edge a tiny stream of water trickled through a small, sandy branch. Whitton led Calhoon to it, they swung down, watered the horses sparingly, splashed water on themselves, as Calhoon gratefully removed the coat and hat. His body felt as if it had been flailed with a cat-o'-nine-tails, and his pants were shredded. But forever the cavalryman, his first thought was for his horse.

The animal was bleeding from dozens of cuts and scrapes, its forequarters especially quilled with thorns. Some slipped out easily, others were barbed and would not come out at all. Flies had already gathered on the wounds.

"Hold on a minnit," Whitton said and went to the cabin, which was still roofed. He disappeared inside, came back with a glass jar full of greasy substance. "Lemme have your knife." Calhoon gave it to him. "Now take the cheek strap and hold him tight."

Whitton crooned as he went to work on the Morgan, loosening barbs when he could, shoving others brutally on under the skin. When he was through, he slathered the goo from the jar over the raw spots. "Pine pitch, creosote, melted hawg lard," he said. "My own mixture. Keeps off the flies. He'll heal up after a while." He pointed at his buckskin. "See all them knots on him? He got more thorns under his hide than he got hair in his mane. Flesh gits hard around 'em, he don't feel 'em. Always tell a good brush horse by them thorn knots." He capped the jar, handed it to Calhoon, then swung back up in his own saddle. "Put that back in the cabin. There's some jerky in there in a tin box, too, do you git hungry. Me and Henry, we keep a few things on hand here."

Calhoon said, "Where you think you're going?"

Whitton looked down at him from the saddle, black face expressionless. "I goin' after a witness, somebody to swear I own this horse, keep you and me both from gittin' killed by goin' in to Double Oaks right now. I be back come nightfall, Henry Gannon with me. Meantime, you might wanta use some of that pine tar on yo'self. You look like a man lost a fight with a good-sized bobcat."

Calhoon hesitated. "I'm not sure—"

"Awright," Whitton said. "You keep me here then, as your prisoner. I try to run, you shoot me. Then you find your way outa this brush yourself. Or tomorrow you make me lead you out. Only, I can lose you before you know what's happenin', and you can wander in this shinnery until you die." Then his taut body relaxed a little. "Man, you took a rope off my neck. Maybe I ain't said thanks,

but you don't have to worry. I be back, me and Henry. I
think the two of you strike it off. Matter of fact, things
break right, what you did back yonder jest might make
you rich, if it don't make you dead." Then he whirled his
mount and galloped across the clearing, back insolently
exposed to Calhoon.

Calhoon stood there motionless, watched him go. Whitton disappeared into the scrub. When he had vanished,
Calhoon grunted a rueful curse. "Rich," he said. "Rich.
Or dead. Hell." He went down to the stream and, with his
guns close at hand, stripped, washed, and used some of
Whitton's pine pitch. It burned like fire and smelled like
the devil, but it made the cuts feel better.

He found the jerky, like thin strips of leather, ate a little. Under the live oaks it was cooler, and cooler yet inside
the cabin, which was obviously used as an occasional
camp and a cache for a few supplies. Some blankets, a can
of powder, a box of percussion caps for a revolver, the
pine pitch medicine, and in one corner, a branding iron
leaning against the wall. It was heavy, the design on its
end big and intricate. Calhoon picked it up, pressed it into
the dust on the floor. It made a large $\underset{B}{R}$.

Calhoon went outside, sat down with his back against
an oak trunk, the rifle across his knees, while the Morgan
cropped grass. Tired as he was, he remained wholly alert,
and more than once he heard sounds from the thickets
that rimmed him on all sides. As the sun heeled down the
sky, there was more noise in the brush from all sides; once
a longhorn cow, roan and gaunt, loped out of the brush,
saw him there, halted, startled, then turned and fled, tail
curled high. Another time two bulls emerged, one huge
and brindle, the other smaller, black. Like the cow, they
spotted Calhoon, but they did not run as swiftly. The
smaller one shied off; the big one put his head down,
pawed the dirt with a splayed hoof, scraping up dust and
throwing it back over his shoulders. There was a moment
when Calhoon expected a charge and raised the Henry;
then the big animal thought better of it and backed into

the thicket, silently as a snake. Calhoon grinned faintly,
relaxed a little. He knew what those sounds were now; cattle coming down to the branch to water.

Then he heard another sound, and this one brought him
to his feet. He cocked his head, listened carefully. His eyes
flickered to the Morgan. It stood, head up, ears pricked
forward. Then it nickered softly.

Horses coming, riders. Maybe Whitton and his friend,
maybe not. Calhoon dodged inside the cabin, watched the
Morgan's head and the brush toward which it pointed. He
had the Henry raised, cradled on the sill of a glassless window. Then a deep voice called, not loudly, but in a tone
that carried, "Yo. Calhoon."

He did not answer, only waited. Long ago he'd learned
to take nothing for granted where survival was concerned;
and in this country that went double. He did not relax his
watchfulness one bit until Elias Whitton emerged from the
thicket, followed by another rider. And even then, when
Calhoon went to meet them, walking toward them under
the oaks, he kept the Henry cradled in his right arm's
crook and his hand very close to the Colt.

Whitton reined in the buckskin, swung down. The man
behind him followed suit, dismounting from a small, wiry
bay. He was white, as tall as Calhoon, and as wide in the
shoulders, but thicker in the chest. He had hardly any
waist or hips at all, and his long legs were lean and slightly
bowed. As he strode forward, big spurs jingling on his
heels, the sun glinted on a shag of fiery red hair curling
from beneath his narrow-brimmed, flat-crowned hat. He
was, Calhoon judged, not over thirty, and he had a face so
ugly it was nearly handsome, like something chopped out
of hard wood with a dull hatchet. His eyes were blue, his
grin wide as, evidently having been forewarned by Whitton, he put out his left hand for Calhoon to take. Calhoon
saw that he wore an old Starr revolver, Confederate Army
issue, on each hip; and that Whitton, too, was armed
again. It was with some hesitation that he yielded his fighting hand to the other's grip.

"So you're Calhoon. I'm Henry Gannon. What's the front end of your handle? 'Lias couldn't recollect."

"Lucius. Lucius Calhoon."

Gannon's hand was big and hard. He squeezed, then let go, backed off a pace, raked Calhoon up and down with his eyes. Saw the gray hat and pants and asked, "Cavalry? What outfit."

"Hampton's South Carolina, Black Horse Troop."

"Me, I rode with Hood. Welcome to Rancho Bravo, Calhoon."

Whitton said, "I'll make a fire, git some chuck cooked 'fore dark. We won't want no blaze after nightfall." He moved off, gathering dead brush, which he carried into the cabin.

Gannon strode over to an oak, squatted on his heels in the shade. Calhoon joined him, still looking him over carefully, liking what he saw: the ugly but open and frank face dusted with freckles, the smooth, quick way Gannon moved. Gannon took from his pocket a tobacco pouch and brown cigarette papers. His eyes flicked to Calhoon's wrist. "You don't mind another man's spit, I'll roll you one."

"I'll just borrow the makings," Calhoon said.

Gannon watched him narrowly, saw how he used the single hand and his teeth, wasting no tobacco, turning out a neat cylinder with a tightly twisted end. When Calhoon had it in his mouth and had passed back the stuff, Gannon said, "'Lias told me you were good with that one hand. I'll say he's right. Where'd you lose the other?"

"Belle Isle," Calhoon said.

Surprise flickered in Gannon's eyes. "Hell, that was a Yankee prison."

"Yeah," Calhoon said tersely and added nothing. Gannon fished out a match, struck it on his thumb, and lit the cigarette, then rolled another for himself. When they were smoking, he said, "I appreciate what you did for 'Lias."

"There's still the question of the horse," Calhoon said.

"The buckskin? Hell, everybody knows Elias raised him from a colt. You got my word on that, and I'll testify in court if it comes to that. But it won't. Not even Isaacs has got nerve enough to try to take that horse any way but what he did—bushwhackin' a man on a lonely road."

"All right," Calhoon said. "I'll take your word. That settles the matter of the horse."

"Yeah. Elias says you was bound for Double Oaks. Any special purpose?"

Calhoon did not answer.

"A lot of people . . ." Gannon was not looking at him now. "A lot of people drifting into Texas these days. Some looking to make a fortune. Only maybe you already got a fortune."

"No," Calhoon said. "I have no fortune. I'm dead broke." He paused. "I had a plantation in South Carolina. Sherman burnt everything on it when he marched through. The land was mortgaged, and by the time I got home, it was gone. I had enough cotton stored to pay the mortgage, but the local Treasury agent had already confiscated it as Confederate contraband, sold it at auction, put the money in his own pocket. So—" He gestured. "I've got what's on me and in my bedroll and the Morgan. And maybe two bits in silver."

Gannon laughed harshly. "Then you're as loaded with cash as I am." Suddenly his face went sober, and he looked at Calhoon keenly. "But you are a fighting man," he said. " 'Lias testifies to that. Anybody that was an officer with Hampton had to be, anyhow."

"I had three years of it," Calhoon said. "And then one year in prison."

"All the same, 'Lias says you're as good with that left hand as most men are with two. He told me about the buckshot in that leather on your right, too. A man don't load something like that on his arm without he's expecting to fight some more."

"I didn't figure I'd get through the rest of my life without fighting again," Calhoon said. "After I lost the hand, I had plenty of time to think about how a man could get along one-handed. After they turned me loose, I took some time to practice. I can do some things one-handed, yeah. Some things I can't."

"If you can fight, that's enough for now." Gannon paused. "What do they call you, Lucius? Luke? Loosh?"

"Loosh is good enough."

Gannon stood up, dribbled smoke through his nostrils, dropped the cigarette end, and ground it out. He was silent for a moment. Then he said, "Maybe you would be interested in a proposition. Likely not an easy one for a man with your handicap and a lot to learn. But the main thing is, you're a Rebel like myself—"

"No," said Calhoon, "I'm not a Rebel."

Gannon stared at him. "But—"

Calhoon stood up, too, and ducked his own cigarette. "I was a kid when South Carolina seceded," he said. "I didn't know a damn thing about States' Rights or politics or anything except that there was a war and I wanted to be in the middle of it because I had so much piss and vinegar in me I couldn't stand it. Well, I had my fighting, and I got whipped. A man has a lot of time to think in prison, Gannon. I thought and I thought, but one of the things I never could figure out was why white men were killing each other over *them*." He pointed at Whitton, who came out of the cabin for more wood. "They ain't worth it, none of them. We had two hundred slaves, and when they went, I said good riddance, and I meant it. I just wish they had never been brought over from Africa in the first place." He spat. "I have got to the point where I hate the sight of 'em, and if the Yankees want 'em, they're welcome to 'em. I'm only sorry so many men had to die and so much be lost before we turned 'em loose and got 'em off our necks."

Gannon blinked. "But you went up against Isaacs to—"

"It was four against one and murder. I'm not built so I can stand by and watch that. But it doesn't change the way I feel about 'em."

Gannon rubbed his face. "Then maybe we'd best forget about the proposition. Because 'Lias is my partner in it."

"Your partner? You mean equal?"

"I mean equal. Without him I couldn't carry it off. Black or white, he's a lot of man, Calhoon."

"That's not the way I heard Texans looked at it."

"It's the way I look at it. The past six months, 'Lias and I've put in a lot of hard work together. I've seen him tail down a bull that was about to punch a horn clean through me. You hunt cattle in the brush with another man, the two of you got to rely on each other or you're dead or crippled. I rely on Elias Whitton. Besides, like I said, without him I can't make it work." His blue eyes glittered. "And I aim to make it work, Weymouth or no Weymouth. I aim to make it work, and I aim to get rich."

"Rich," said Calhoon. "He used that word, too."

"Or dead."

"And that one," Calhoon said. His eyes went to Whitton again, striding into the cabin with another load of wood. "And you said another name. Weymouth."

"He's the man we'll have to fight before we're through."

Calhoon was silent for a moment. "That might make a d'fference," he said. "Suppose you tell me what you got in mind, Henry Gannon. If it combines fighting Weymouth and getting rich both, I just might link up with the devil himself, black or white."

Chapter 3

Not far away in the brush, a bull bellowed, challenging another to combat. Henry Gannon looked appraisingly at Lucius Calhoon, a keen intelligence working behind his eyes. "Weymouth," he said. "You have got a mad against him?"

Calhoon stood up. "For now that's my affair. But let's say, yes—I've business with Gordon Weymouth."

Gannon's eyes went to the Colt .36 on Calhoon's hip, the hilt of the knife protruding from his boot. "Hard business, I'd say from the look of it. Well, you have the same kind with Josh Weymouth too, now. Isaacs is Weymouth's man, and you've crossed him. Besides, there is nothing Josh Weymouth would have liked better than to see Elias Whitton danglin' from that limb, dead as a doornail." He rubbed his jaw thoughtfully. "Yeah, you're in this anyhow, Calhoon. Up to your ears, whether you want to be or not."

"Into what?"

"It's a long story, and I'll have to start from the beginning."

"I have time," Calhoon said.

"Sho." Gannon flung out one arm in a sweeping gesture. "Well, to boil it down, this is my range, Calhoon. You start from here, ride any direction, it'll be midnight anyhow before you hit my boundary."

"A big place," Calhoon said, grappling with the magnitude of such ownership.

"My daddy was a drover by trade, came down from Tennessee and helped old Sam Houston grab this state away from Mexico. Grabbed all of this brush country he could get hold of, too. Even then it was alive with cow-critters, wild Spanish stock, and he saw 'em as dollars on

29

the hoof, so he let the farmers have the open country. He hunted out cows, drove 'em along the old Beef Trail to New Orleans, shipped some by boat to Cuba, made himself a fortune, and never made but one mistake in his whole life—he put his money in Confederate currency and Confederate bonds, every penny."

Gannon paused. "Anyhow, I come home from the war the last of the family, Daddy dead and my brother Lee killed outside Atlanta. While I was gone, our stock multiplied like rabbits. Thousands of longhorns gone wild here, no man's put rope on 'em for near five years. So that was all I had, Calhoon. The land and all those unmarked cattle." His mouth twisted. "Now I'm gonna lose the land."

"Lose it how?"

"Taxes," Gannon said. "I don't know how it is in South Carolina, Calhoon, but down here we got a provisional governor appointed by Andrew Johnson until we draw up a new constitution and it's approved by Congress and we get back into the Union. Well, the governor, he's appointed men to fill the county offices, Union men like himself naturally; Texans who sided with the North. Josh Weymouth was one of those, and now he's county judge and tax assessor and has all his own men in the other county offices. On top of that, he's federal Treasury agent for the district, empowered to seize Confederate government property whenever he finds it, with a troop of Yankee cavalry stationed in Double Oaks to back him up on that."

"Go on," Calhoon said.

"Well, Josh Weymouth hates my guts." Gannon grinned ruefully. "And I can't deny that he has good reason. Before Secession, Union sympathizers lived hard around here and Weymouth harder than most, partly because he was so loud mouthed about it, partly because my daddy was the most brass-bound, copper-riveted Secessionist in the county, and he made up his mind to destroy Weymouth or drive him out. He put the pressure on, and Weymouth finally had to run north to Yankee protection. But now he's back, and he can't strike at Daddy, God rest his soul, but he sure as hell can at me. So as county tax assessor, he's hit me for back taxes on my land from 1860 on—two thousand dollars, and if I don't pay it in ninety days, the land goes at public auction. I reckon you can guess who'll buy it."

Calhoon whistled. "A lot of money. You can't pay in cattle?"

Gannon's laugh was bitter. "You can't *give* cattle away in Texas right now. There's no market except in New Orleans, and a man named Abel Pierce has formed a syndicate and sewed that up. Oh, there's talk of driving north to Missouri, but the farmers up there are so afraid of tick fever they'll never let Texas cattle through; that's just a soap bubble." He shook his head. "No, the land's gone. And when it goes, every unbranded cow on it will go along with it, just like the jaybirds and the jackrabbits in the brush. The only ones I can move off the range are those with my iron on them—and, Calhoon, there must be six thousand cattle on this land and not more than a thousand marked!"

Calhoon digested this. "In other words, whoever picks up the land for taxes gets maybe five thousand cattle with it, thrown in free."

"That's the size of it. Like I say, I've got maybe a thousand marked right now and of that thousand about four hundred in pens me and 'Lias have built or herdbroke enough so they'll stay on pasture. And that ain't enough, Calhoon!" Suddenly his eyes flared. "Two thousand, I got to have two thousand at the very least! If I can't get those, Weymouth can have the land and all the rest. But I've got to have two thousand to make me rich!"

Calhoon stared at Gannon. He liked the big, redheaded man, liked the honesty in his face, his straightforward manner. And he felt something radiating from Gannon, a curious power, an intensity. "You said that before. Rich, how—?"

"Come with me," Gannon snapped. He whirled, strode toward the cabin, and Calhoon followed.

Inside it Elias Whitton crouched before the fireplace, turning a loin of beef on a spit over glowing coals. Gannon went to the branding iron Calhoon had picked up earlier, seized and whirled it, holding it high. "You know what this is?"

"A branding iron. RB."

"RB—" Gannon's laugh was short, explosive, as his fingers caressed the curled hieroglyph of steel. In the dimness the firelight danced on his ugly face, struck glints from his blue eyes. "It's more than that, Loosh Calhoon. RB—you know what that stands for? It stands for the empire me and 'Lias Whitton aim to build! It stands for Rancho Bravo!"

The fire popped and hissed as beef fat dripped into the coals. "Rancho Bravo," Calhoon said after a moment. Curiously the words seemed to have a taste; he liked the sound of them.

"That's it. 'Lias. It's your turn now. Tell Calhoon what's out there beyond the Pecos River!"

Calhoon looked at Whitton as the black man gave the spit another turn and then arose. When Whitton spoke, the single word rang in the room like a trumpet note.

"Grass," he said.

Henry Gannon let out a gusty sigh. "That's right, Calhoon—grass! Buffalo and grama both, short grass and tall! An ocean of it, miles of it, far as a man can see, more than he can imagine! All the grass—" his voice rose "—a man could ever need if he has the guts to take and hold it! You understand, Calhoon? It don't matter about this brush—let Weymouth have it. What I want is the grass out yonder! 'Lias, tell him the rest."

"Before the war," Whitton said, "I a slave, you know? Rode for a hard master, breakin' horses and workin' cattle. A ready man with a whip, and I not takin' kindly to bein' whipped, so I run away. Not nawth, where they could catch me. But west, all the way west into Comanche country, where there weren't no white men at all."

Now he seemed to look through Calhoon, to stare into distance. "The *Nuema,* the People, they call theirselves. And it a good thing for me that Comanches love a horse and a man that can handle one. Because they struck my trail and rode me down in relays, same like coyotes after a pronghorn. Only I was mounted on a tough little pinto, and he and me knowed one another, and I outrode 'em. I knowed how to git more outa my horse than they did outa theirs. Oh, sho, they finally got me, but they couldn't believe how much that little paint give me before he played out, and they figured I must have some kind of magic. So even though they don't usually take to black people, they didn't kill me right off; they wanted to find out about my medicine. I mean, we didn't speak each other's language, but we both talked horse, and that saved my hide. Way things fell out, I showed them some tricks, and they showed me some, and they took me into the tribe. I married a Comanche woman, but she died last year, havin' a baby, my baby." His mouth worked. "Baby died, too."

"Anyhow," he went on, "I had heard by then that the freedom had done been passed. Got restless, itchy, seemed to me like I had to come back and see what it feel like to walk free among the whites. Had a notion, too, to settle an old score with that old master of mine, the whip man. Only, hard times beat me to that, and he so broke and pitiful, sons dead in the war, that I couldn't raise a hand to him."

His eyes narrowed. "This freedom. It all right, but it ain't like the freedom I done had out there on the short grass, where a man can see from one edge of the world plumb to the other. And there too many white folks—" his eyes met Calhoon's "—around that jest don't believe a black man due any freedom regardless of what the gov'ment say. Likely I woulda turned, headed right on back if I hadn't bumped into Henry. But he needed somebody to he'p him with his cattle, and then Weymouth come down on him. All of a sudden he find out he gonna lose his land, and there he is with cows and no grass. Me, I know where there all the grass in the world and no cows. So he and I make our plan, and it this: we git our herd together, and we drive it west, across the Pecos. That Comanche country, sure, but I a Comanche, too, and I can deal with 'em. We handle it right, pay 'em with cattle and trade goods and treat 'em decent, we can git grazin' rights and protection against the other tribes." Suddenly he drew his sheath knife, squatted, and sketched lines in the dust of the floor.

"Here," he said, "the Pecos, runnin' slantwise, northwest to southeast. Down here the Big Bend of the Rio Grande—Rio Bravo, the Mes'cans call it—and at the bottom part, it all desert and badlands. But up above, here beyond the Pecos, there a high plateau, good water, and that where the grass begins. And it run on for miles, north, west, anywhere you want to look. So far, nobody dared to touch it on account of Comanches. We'd be the first—"

"You see, Calhoon?" Gannon cut in excitedly. "With two thousand head we'll git there first and stake out the biggest ranch in Texas! On top of that, in a year we'll have a hundred thousand in gold to work with."

Calhoon stared at him. "A hundred thousand—?"

"Hell, yes! The mines of Colorado!" Gannon gestured. "Five years now, while the war went on, they been out there diggin' gold and silver outa the Rockies by the bucketful! And all that time, damned little beef to eat, a smidgen from California, a dab from Utah, no more! Calhoon, those miners are starvin' for meat, and they got gold to pay for it. A lousy longhorn you can't give away here'd bring seventy dollars on the hoof in Denver City. Look—" He drew with the branding iron. "We deal with the Comanches, stake out our range here above the Big Bend, drop off young she-stuff and a few bulls, drive the rest across New Mexico on up to Denver! Sell it off, collect our gold, come back here, buy another herd, do it again! Then the Army—sooner or later it'll move back to the frontier. It'll need beef, too, and we'll be the only ones there to supply it! I tell you, Calhoon, with two thousand head, some guts and luck, we can build the biggest ranch in Texas and make a fortune!"

His voice trailed off. For a moment the cabin was silent. "We," Calhoon said at last. "You keep saying we. Where do I come in?"

"Why," Henry Gannon said, "we need a man like you! Me and 'Lias talked it over. You come in with us, and we'll give you ten percent!"

Lucius Calhoon looked from the tall, rangy redhead to the squat, black figure of Elias Whitton. "Need me—why?" he said at last.

"It my idea," Elias Whitton said. "Today you save my life. I look for some way to pay you back. And Henry owe you jest as big a debt, because Rancho Bravo won't work without me. Next thing is, it don't matter about that hand. The left one is what counts. I seen many a two-handed fightin' man, red, black, white, but before today never one could take me when I come after him. You got that left hand and guns to use in it, you got nerve and judgment. All that pay your way."

"Calhoon," Henry Gannon cut in earnestly, "there ain't but the two of us, me and 'Lias. We need more riders, a lot of 'em, but we got no cash to pay 'em with. So it's up to me and Whitton to gouge as many cattle out of this brush as we can before the deadline. Only, we got to have somebody to cover us while we do it." He shook his head. "Every cow we brand is one more Josh Weymouth doesn't git. Maybe he's got no use for 'em himself, but he begrudges 'em to me all the same. And he's got Isaacs and thirty, forty men to block our cow hunt. You saw what nearly happened to 'Lias this afternoon! He's not about to let us go on with our roundup without makin' us fight! Every gun we can get on our side is that much in our favor." He paused. "We can't pay you, either, except a percentage. But if you'll throw in with us, do what you can, help us stand against Weymouth, you'll get ten percent of Rancho Bravo. Ten percent of the land, the stock, whatever gold we get in Colorado." He thrust with the branding iron as with a saber. "You're busted like we are, like everybody is. You got a grudge against Weymouth somehow, and Weymouth's got one against you. Like I told you, we're offerin' you a chance to get back on your feet, be part of somethin' big, the biggest thing Texas has ever seen—and work out your mad on Weymouth at the same time. You don't know us, we don't know you, but we're in the same boat, and we got the same enemies, and that counts for a lot." He took a step forward. "Rancho Bravo, Calhoon! I've registered it legal as a new brand in addition to the old one my daddy had of J Bar G! Some-day it'll be known all over the whole damn West and so will the men who own it! So— What do you say, Cal-hoon? You want in? We'll gamble if you will!"

"Rancho Bravo," Calhoon repeated, and again it had a fine sound, almost a taste to it. But then, slowly he shook his head.

"No," he said.

Henry Gannon let the branding iron drop.

Elias Whitton rasped out a gusty sigh. "Awright," he said. "You the big master, and I the nigger slave. That what gravel you?"

Calhoon looked at him. "Maybe," he said harshly. "I am accustomed to doing business with white men."

"I figgered that," Whitton said tautly.

"But that's not it," Calhoon said. He looked from one of them to the other. "You're right," he said. "I'm dead broke. I've lost everything I ever owned and maybe every-thing I ever believed in. A man in my position can't afford to be choosy, and I've told Gannon that I'd work with the devil himself to strike out at Weymouth. But Joshua— You're talking about the wrong man. It's not the father I want. It's the son I've come a thousand miles to find. Gor-don. My business is with him. I hear he's in Double Oaks, and I have time for nothing else except finding him and killing him."

"Ahhh . . ." It was a kind of sigh Henry Gannon let out after a moment. "I thought that was it." His eyes shuttled to the maimed right wrist. "Having to do with that?"

Calhoon did not answer directly. "Is Gordon in Double Oaks?"

"Was, the last I heard," Gannon said.

"Then," said Calhoon, "that's it. I don't want ten per-cent of your Rancho Bravo. All I want's a meal of that beef, a place to sleep, and to be guided out again to the main road to town tomorrow morning. You give me that, we're square for this afternoon."

"Man," Whitton said after a moment's pause, "you're crazy."

"That's entirely possible," Calhoon said. "But not crazier than you two. To think you can round up two thousand cattle and drive 'em west alone."

"That ain't it," Whitton said. "You don't understand. Isaacs and all his men be in Double Oaks, more than thirty of them bushwhackers from up in Kansas and Missouri. They Weymouth's people, and they know you now, and you never git through to Gordon." He turned and spat into the fire. "You be dead before you halfway down the street."

"I won't be dead before I get Gordon Weymouth," Calhoon said, "I promise you that much. Nobody is gonna stop me—" His vo_ce rose. "Nobody—" Suddenly it seemed that his right hand ached, though there was no right hand there. "By God," he heard himself saying loudly, "I've had enough, you understand? You leave one government and form another, and it's just as bad. You charge the goddamn guns, and the infantry don't come up! You get captured and think you're through with all of it, and then they string you up by your wrists—"

"Weymouth did that to you?" Gannon cut in.

"He did it to me!" Now Calhoun no longer cared, everything bottled up inside him pouring out. "They took me during the retreat from Gettysburg, when my horse got shot out from under me. And . . . it was a relief. I was tired of war, didn't believe in it any longer, white men killing each other over—" He looked at Whitton, broke off.

"So they put me in Belle Isle," he went on, voice lower now. "A hell hole, yeah, but I could have made it all the same. Only there was this lieutenant, a Texan who'd joined the Union Army and was sittin' out the war in a nice, safe job. And thought he could prove how much man he still was by hurting people who couldn't fight back. I called the son of a bitch on it, made complaint over his head to h_s superior. It d_dn't work, and he found out about it. So . . . he put me in a punishment cell. Stark naked, strung up there for two days by my wrists, feet barely on the floor, no food or water . . ."

"God Almig_ty," whispered Gannon.

"You cut off the circulation long enough," Calhoon said

with curious dispassion, "and gangrene sets in. When they finally cut me down, my right hand was black as coal, and the stink would turn your gut. So they took me to the surgeons . . ."

Now his voice turned harsh. "Only the surgeons were short of opium, you see? Grant's big offensive took all they had, none to waste on Rebel prisoners. I got a shot of whiskey and a piece of wood covered with leather to bite down on, and then they cut off the hand. I . . . felt it. You're damn well told I felt it . . ."

"Judas Priest." Gannon's mouth worked.

"Even at that I nearly died. I had a long time in the place they called the hospital—hog pen was more like it—to think. And the only thing that brought me through was the thought of what I was gonna to do to that lieutenant when the war was over. But by the time I was well, he'd been transferred somewhere else, and then the war ended, and I went home to South Carolina. There was nothing left there, nothing. They'd taken it all. But . . . it didn't matter, you see? I didn't want it anymore, didn't care about it. All I wanted was *him*."

Instinctively he touched his holstered Colt. "I taught myself to use my left hand and use it good. I trailed that bastard, and now I've found him. If he's in Double Oaks, by tomorrow night one or the other or maybe both of us will be dead. So you see? Even if I wanted to, I wouldn't be much use to you and your Rancho Bravo. A dead man or one on the run can't use ten percent of anything."

He stopped then, and neither Henry Gannon nor Elias Whitton said a word. They only looked at him in a kind of awe. And during that interval sanity, as much as he ever had of it now, returned to Lucius Calhoon. He turned away. "Anyhow," he said, "the two of you are crazy as I am. It won't work, your Rancho Bravo."

"You think not?" Henry Gannon asked hoarsely.

Calhoon turned back to face him, and now his voice was level, almost gentle. "How can it? Two men with only ninety days to round up more than a thousand head of cattle? And then what? Drive them hundreds of miles through Indian country?" He shook his head. "No, Gannon. All you're gonna do is break your heart."

Henry Gannon's big hands gripped the branding iron. "You think so, eh? Well, let me tell you something, Loosh Calhoon. I'm gonna *make* it work! If me and 'Lias have to go it alone, by God, if we have to drive those cows on foot and herd 'em with ox goads, we're gonna do it." He sucked in a breath. "First there was only me and all that brush and the cattle. And even then I had a dream. Then come Elias, and he showed me how to make that dream real. So now there are two of us and the start of a herd, and somehow or another, before the deadline comes, there'll be more: more men, more cattle. Don't ask me how, because I can't tell you. All I know is, it's true." He held out the branding iron. "Because it's big, Calhoon. Rancho Bravo. It's so big that nothing can stop it, nobody! You hear?"

Again the cabin fell silent. Presently Calhoon said quietly, "I hear. Maybe I was wrong. But anyhow, I'm going to do what I have to do. And all I'll trouble you for is a meal, a place to unroll my blankets, and directions to Double Oaks in the morning."

Chapter 4

Shimmering in the heat, the town lay spread out below him as he topped a rise.

He did not stop to look at it until he was on the forward slope; instinct would not let him sit still, skylined.

For a county seat it was not much; but none of these backwoods Texas towns were. A scattering of squalid huts, mostly mud with thatched roofs, and that would be the Mexican quarter; further along the single, wide, dusty street some more substantial houses of log or frame; and then a few stores, saloons and businesses, the whole thing ending in a plaza shaded by ancient cottonwoods. On the far side of that was the biggest structure in Double Oaks, two stories, made of logs: the county courthouse. And it was there, Calhoon thought, that Henry Gannon had told him he would likely find Gordon Weymouth. "If he ain't there," Gannon had continued, "look for him at The Texas Flag. That's the saloon where Isaacs and his men hang out."

Now Calhoon's hand tightened on the Henry. He had another quarter mile of dusty road to cover before he reached the town, and then he would sheathe the rifle and rely on the handgun and the knife in his boot. His mouth felt dry, his whole body tautly stretched, and he was aware of the pounding of his heart. After all this time, all the long miles of travel, soon the game would be in sight. Suddenly impatient, he touched spurs to the Morgan and sent it galloping down the slope. As he had all the way from Henry Gannon's ranch, he watched his flanks and back-trail constantly.

The three of them had spent the night at the tumbled-down cabin, while longhorns moaned in the brush. There

41

had been beef and branch water, nothing else; Gannon lacked cash even for coffee, which was scarce and expensive anyhow, or for flour. After the meal there had been more talk; Gannon, at Calhoon's request, sketching out the situation in Double Oaks.

"It's all mixed up," he had said. "Josh Weymouth is the civil authority, the top dog there. But the military authority's in the hands of Philip Killraine. He's the bluebelly captain that commands the cavalry troop."

"Killraine a good man," Whitton had put in. "Don't you low-rate him. Our goose already be cooked, it weren't for Killraine."

"He's all right for a Yankee." There had been grudging admiration in Gannon's voice. "You see, Calhoon, nobody knows where Weymouth's authority leaves off and Killraine's begins. Right now we're not exactly under military occupation and yet maybe we are a little. Weymouth's supposed to run the county and his sheriff and deputies enforce the civil laws. Killraine's soldiers are supposed to keep general peace and order and make sure the freedmen, the exslaves like Elias here, git a fair shake. Plus, anything Weymouth does as federal Treasury agent, Killraine's got to back him up. But the two of them—well, it's a break for us that Killraine don't like Weymouth any better than I do. He came in here with his soldiers, and Weymouth assumed Killraine would help him steal the county blind and git his revenge on everybody he had a grudge against. But when Killraine saw what Weymouth was about, he backed off and hard. He's a West Pointer, one of them with a ramrod for a backbone, and even though he's got no love for Texans and Confederates in general, he's honest as hell, I'll give him that. So he said no to Weymouth when Weymouth wanted him to use his soldiers for what Killraine figgered was improper purposes, and he and Weymouth been at each other's throats ever since. Or at least Weymouth's been at his."

"I see." Calhoon had nodded.

"Then, not long ago Weymouth give up on Killraine and brought in Isaacs and his Regulators. Like 'Lias told you, they're nothin' but bushwhackers and guerrilla fighters from up on the Kansas-Missouri border. What they really are is Weymouth's private army, to smash down anybody in this county who gets in his way. What they were tryin' to do to Elias when you caught 'em—well, I reckon that's their first move against us. Likely there'll be more before very long. That all depends on whether or not Killraine lets 'em hang around or cracks down on 'em. Anyhow, they're what Weymouth will be sending against us, and they're what you're gonna have to plough through somehow to get Gordon Weymouth."

"I'll get him," was all Calhoon had said.

"Maybe," Gannon had said. "Likely it'll cost you dear."

"I'm prepared to pay," Calhoon had said and then had rolled up in his blankets.

The next morning Henry and Elias had led him along winding trails through the brush, across great pastures that were by comparison clear and open. Finally they had come to a big frame house in a clearing, beneath huge live oaks and surrounded by outbuildings and corrals. Before riding up to it, though, they had paused in the brush, and Whitton had slid from his buckskin, gone ahead on foot, gun ready, disappearing into cover like a wisp of fog. Not much time had passed before he loped back. "All clear. They come lookin' for us last night, then rode away."

"Didn't harm the house?" Gannon had asked.

Whitton had grinned sardonically. "You know Weymouth not allow that when it belong to him in ninety days anyhow."

From Gannon's homeplace, which this was, a wagon road led south. "Follow that," Henry had said, "and it'll take you to the main road to Double Oaks." He had paused. "You won't reconsider, Loosh?"

Calhoon had only shrugged.

"Well—" Henry's face had been serious. He had thrust out his left hand. "Good luck."

"Yeah," Whitton had said, putting his buckskin up close. "You gonna need it." He had made a tentative gesture with his left hand, then had let it drop. "However it fall out, remember this: I in your debt. And that offer we made you, is still open any time."

"Thanks," Calhoon had said and, then with impatience in him, had turned the Morgan and set off down the road.

Now, as he entered the street, passing through the Mexican quarter, he slowed the horse. He sheathed the rifle and wrapped the reins loosely around his right wrist and let his left dangle by the holstered Navy, the loads and caps of which he had checked and rechecked. He no longer allowed himself the luxury of emotion but, seemingly frozen inside, rode with every sense focused and alert and every muscle tensed for action. First the courthouse, he thought; and then, if he did not find Gordon there, The Texas Flag.

There was not much traffic on the street: a couple of civilian horsemen who looked at him with brief curiosity; a wagon, its white tarp stenciled *USA*, jangled by, drawn by fat, well-curried mules. But there were a lot of animals at the hitchracks ahead in the business section, and Calhoon slowed the horse to a walk, head swiveling from side to side, searching the porches of the stores and saloons for the one face he sought, the one forever engraved in his memory.

And every porch had its considerable throng of men. Cut from the same cloth as Henry Gannon, they lounged in idleness, bearded, hungry looking, clad in leather or the remnants of Confederate uniforms or both. "They're like me," Gannon had said of them. "Without a penny in their pockets and nobody got the money to hire 'em on. When they want to eat, they go out in the *brasada* and kill a maverick; rest of the time they jest set and set, waitin' for somethin' to happen, but they don't know what . . . I offered 'em top wages when we sell the herd in Colorado, but they jest laughed at me. Thought I was crazy, same as you do. Besides, they got to have somethin' now . . ."

They were no novelty to Calhoon. He had seen their like everywhere he had been in the South; men whose trade for four years had been fighting; beaten men, come home to poverty and ruination, hope squeezed out of them. As he rode by, they watched him with guarded curiosity, and he saw that more than one of them was, like himself, minus a hand . . . or an arm or leg.

Then, up ahead he saw the sign: THE TEXAS FLAG. Isaacs' hangout and Gordon Weymouth's. His hand tightened on the Colt, and he sat straighter in the saddle. There were men on the porch of this saloon, too, but of a different cut: better fed, better clad, and armed to the teeth, each with at least one side gun, most with two, some with bandoliers across their chests. These were fighters, too, but of a different kind, bearing the predatory, hard-bitten stamp of the border bushwhacker, the guerrilla . . . They watched Calhoon come, and all ten or twelve of them moved closer to the porch's edge. He stared back at them directly, looking for that face among them, but did not see it; nor was Isaacs there. Then he had passed by. He turned in his saddle and looked back; a man spat into the dust, and they kept on watching him, but no one moved.

Letting the Morgan out a little, he trotted the rest of the way across the plaza and to the courthouse. There only a blue-clad guard at the doorway watched him curiously as he swung down, tied the horse. Calhoon paused before the high steps for a moment, heart pounding; it was a little hard to breathe. Maybe this was it; maybe this was trail's end. Keeping his left flank away from the guard, he loosened the Colt in its holster. *Ten seconds,* he thought. *That's all it'll take. Long enough for me to say my name. Long enough for him to remember. Because I want him to know why. I want him to know and know too that he will die . . .* He sucked in a long breath, went up the steps, strode across the wide porch.

He entered the courthouse and found himself in a long, dim corridor that ran the building's length. There were doors on either side, open because of the heat. Above them little signs jutted out to identify the offices. Calhoon's lips thinned as he read one: Joshua Weymouth — County Judge. It was at the far end of the hall. With his eyes fastened on it, he started forward—and almost collided with the girl who came out of the door right beside him.

"Oh!" she said. "I beg your pardon."

Calhoon backed up a step, touched his hat, dropping his gaze to her. "Excuse me . . ." he said, and then his voice dwindled off as he found himself staring directly into a pair of large green eyes beneath long lashes. They were the most marvelous eyes he had ever seen, and he felt immediate physical impact as he met them.

The girl was young, not much over twenty, auburn hair piled high on her head, glinting with copper lights in the sun streaming through the door. Her nose was straight, small, her mouth full and wide and red, her chin firm, her skin pale; she was, he thought, exceedingly beautiful. She wore an absurd little green hat that was part of a riding costume, and the rest of the dress modeled itself to a full-bosomed, slender-waisted torso which vanished into wide skirts. She carried a riding crop in one hand.

Under Calhoon's stare her cheeks took on color. She looked at his tall, dusty, ragged frame, the gaunt face scarred with brushmarks, and she stared, too, at the Colt on his hip. This time it was she who took a step backward.

Then a man in blue came out of the door just behind her. He was short, his coloring the same as the girl's, and he wore a bristling, auburn cavalry moustache, waxed at the ends. On the epaulets of his uniform were the silver bars of a captain, and his hat bore the crossed sabers of the cavalry. "Evelyn—" he began, then broke off as he saw Calhoon.

"Is there something I can do for you, sir?" This, Calhoon knew, had to be Philip Killraine, commander of the cavalry detachment; his voice was crisp, his accent sharp edged, obviously New England. He looked at Calhoon with a mixture of curiosity and suspicion.

Calhoon glanced down the hall, then back at the captain. "Yes, sir," he said, trying very hard to be casual. "If you can tell me where I might find Mr. Gordon Weymouth."

"Gordon? Or Joshua, his father?"

"It's Gordon I'm looking for."

"Oh," said Killraine. "Well, maybe his father can help you. But Gordon's not here. As I understand it—" and there was a curious hardness in his voice "—he's gone to Washington."

For a moment Lucius Calhoon stood absolutely frozen; he did not even breathe, and his mind seemed to have locked itself tightly, refusing to work. He was, in that instant, wholly blank and then he heard himself repeat the single word, *Washington?*

"That's right," Killraine said sharply. His eyes searched Calhoon's face, narrowing. Almost instinctively he moved in front of the girl, as if to block and shield her from any rash action by this wild-looking wreck of a man.

"Washington," Calhoon said again; this time it came out as a croak. He shook his head, and then slowly his wits returned. It took every ounce of self-control he could muster to keep from cursing or slamming his fist into the wall.

"He left a week ago," Killraine went on. "For an indefinite stay, as I understand it. But," he gestured, "you can get the details from Joshua Weymouth, his father, right down there in the county judge's office. If you're a friend of Gordon's, he'll give you his address, I'm sure."

Calhoon sucked in air, let it out in a long sigh. *Washington. A week . . .* By now Gordon Weymouth would already be on a ship or train . . . Out of his reach. He had spent his last penny, used up all his resources, to come this far and now— "You're sure," he rasped.

"If you doubt my word," Killraine said with irritation, "go ask Judge Weymouth. But I saw him get on the stage to Galveston myself. From there to New Orleans and then by train—"

"No," Calhoon said numbly. "No, I don't doubt your word, Captain. I don't doubt it at all." He stood there motionless, not, for the moment, knowing what to do. Killraine's eyes never left him. Then a voice from Killraine's office broke the taut silence. "Captain, before you go—"

"All right, Temple, I'm coming. Evelyn—" Killraine took the girl's arm. "A few more minutes before we leave. You'd better come back inside and wait."

"Yes, Phil," the girl said, but she was still looking at Calhoon with curiosity as the captain drew her back inside his office and closed the door.

When it shut, Calhoon stood there for perhaps five seconds longer. Then he turned, and now what he felt was not frustration and disappointment but fury—a deep, swiftly growing rage at fate itself. All these months, all these miles, and a week, a rotten, lousy week— The fury exploded within him, exactly like that of a starving animal crouched for the kill, then balked of its prey. He whirled, almost blinded by it, strode toward the courthouse door, crossed the porch. And then he halted.

At the foot of the courthouse steps, Tod Isaacs waited, ginger beard split in a grin. Behind him were ranged a dozen men armed with rifles. As Calhoon stared down at them, they tilted up the barrels to cover him.

"Hello, Reb," Isaacs said.

Under the menace of all those guns Calhoon stood frozen; but curiously he felt no fear. Instead, the rage within him changed to a wild savage joy.

"Isaacs."

"That's right." Then, as the guard at the courthouse door stepped forward, Isaacs snapped, "You there, soldier. Don't you move. I'd hate for you to git hit by a stray bullet!" He turned back to Calhoon. "Come down here, Reb." He backed away a little, his men moving likewise and forming a semicircle.

Calhoon hesitated only a second. Then, grinning himself, he came down the steps. In the dust at their bottom, he confronted Isaacs. "Where's the nigger horsethief, Reb?" Isaacs asked.

"Why," Calhoon said easily, "Henry Gannon proved to me that the buckskin was Whitton's own. So I left him where he was, having no intention of turning him over to the likes of you."

"The likes of me." Isaacs' face darkened. "What would that be, crip?"

"A lot of things," said Calhoon. "None of 'em I'd want to step in."

"Well, then," Isaacs said. "You broke your promise. That makes you the nigger horsethief's accomplice." Suddenly his grin vanished. "Take him, boys!"

They were in on Calhoon with the rifles before he could move. Suddenly Isaacs' hand shot out, whisked Calhoon's gun from holster. "Now we'll take you before Judge Weymouth."

Calhoon's mouth twisted. "You like the odds on your side, don't you?"

"A smart man always does."

Calhoon said happily, "Then what about two hands against one?"

Isaacs stared, eyes dropping to the leather-bound stump. "Meaning?"

"Maybe you'd like to settle what you've got against me right here. If you're not afraid to take off that gun."

"Why," Isaacs said, surprised, "you mean fists? Knuckle and skull? And you a cripple?"

"Don't let that bother you," Calhoon grinned.

"Well, now," Isaacs said. "Well, now, that might be the best way of all. I was sort of hoping you'd resist so we could work you over. And now you ask fer it yourself." He raised his head. "You up there!" he bellowed at the guard on the porch. "You heard it! This here crip wants to fight!" He backed away, handing Calhoon's gun to one man, unbuckling his belt and thrusting the two Army Colts at another. "Spread out, boys," he rasped, "and give us room. Awright, crip, cut loose your wolf!"

"Yeah," Calhoon said, feeling as if he were full of flame. All the frustration and savagery of the morning welled up in him as he looked into Isaacs' face, and he knew now that he was going to do this one-handed, not rely on the shot-loaded right. He wanted to feel his fist on flesh . . . Then he went after Isaacs, and Isaacs came in at him simultaneously.

There was no science in the way they smashed together, only fury, like the collision of two fighting bulls. Calhoon blocked Isaacs' left with his own right arm, and sent his own left smashing toward Isaacs' face. At the same instant Isaacs hit him in the belly Calhoon felt flesh and cartilage give beneath his fist as his first blow broke Isaacs' nose; but the wind went out of him under the impact of Isaacs' right.

Isaacs bellowed, face suddenly streaming scarlet, shoved Calhoon's right aside, smashed at Calhoon blindly. Calhoon blocked with his left, sucked air, struck out, missed, hand sliding off Isaacs' shoulder. Isaacs clubbed both fists, slashed in with tremendous, brutal impact, rocked Calhoon back. He hit and hit again, and Calhoon staggered, fell back on the courthouse steps. Isaacs kicked out hard with a spurred boot.

Calhoon rolled, and the spur raked his cheek. He came up panting and, while Isaacs was still off balance, went for the face once more. Isaacs howled, staggered back, as Calhoon smashed the damaged nose again. Blinded with pain, Isaacs struck out, missed, and Calhoon hit him again, this time in the mouth. Isaacs shook his head wildly, dazed. He tried to back away, but Calhoon closed in, on balance now, with air in his lungs. He used the right wrist to block, chopped in past Isaacs' blind-slugging guard, going always for the face. He connected one more time; hard on the jaw. Isaacs lurched sideways, still spraying blood, and Calhoon whirled to come in after him. This time his fist slid off Isaacs' upraised hands, blocking that damaged, blinded face. Isaacs' simultaneously kicked out, aiming for Calhoon's groin. Just in time, Calhoon caught that thrust on his thigh. Then, wildly, Isaacs slugged at him with right and left, smashed down Calhoon's guard, came in regardless of cost or damage, intent only on battering down Calhoon. Calhoon took punishment, jumped back; Isaacs was, in that split second, open, easy. Calhoon cocked the left, drove it in, and Isaacs ran full into it. As the fist slammed into Isaacs' jaw, Calhoon felt the shock all the way up his arm.

Isaacs swayed, dropped to his knees as if praying. Calhoon laughed, full of killer instinct now, came in hard. As Isaacs reached out to seize his legs, Calhoon brought up a knee. Isaacs' teeth clicked together loudly, and Isaacs rolled over in the dust. Calhoon stepped back, waiting. Isaacs lay there panting. Calhoon fought down the impulse to kick the man, smash him with his boots as Isaacs had tried to do to him when he'd hit the courthouse steps. The world seemed to shimmer through a red mist. Then Isaacs was up on one arm. He raised a face that was a parody of his former features, beard scarlet now with blood, eyes puffed nearly shut. But his voice was loud as he roared: "Ed! Lacy! Take the son of a bitch!"

Calhoon whirled, but he was too late. Now two men closed in on him, armed with rifles. He raised the right wrist with its shotload, but even as he did so, a rifle barrel swept out, slammed against his head. Things went off inside his skull; he felt his knees give way, and he landed on them in the dust. Then hands jerked him to his feet, and suddenly both arms were pinned behind his back. He opened his eyes and saw, through a kind of haze, Isaacs, up now and advancing. And Isaacs was no longer empty handed; in his right he held Calhoon's own gun, barrel straight up. He stood there before Calhoon, face a mask of red, blue eyes shining through it like flakes of ice. His voice was a thick, blood-choked roar. "Now goddamn you, crip, I'm gonna gunwhip the life outa you!"

Calhoon tried to struggle, but he was pinned too tightly. He saw the pistol barrel swinging through the air. He thought simultaneously that he heard a shout from somewhere behind him. But then metal crashed into bone; and for Lucius Calhoon the world exploded.

Chapter 5

Awareness came back in flickering tatters. He knew first the agony in his head, and he felt at the same time the sting of medicine in the cuts and slashes on face and scalp. A voice: "No fracture, maybe slight concussion. But one more blow like that, he'd be in a bad way . . ." He opened his eyes, saw a strange face above him: a man, middle-aged. "Easy," the man said. "I'm a doctor." He dabbed again with the soaked wad of cotton. Calhoon drifted off before the white ball touched his flesh.

When he came to again, he saw no one above him; only canvas; he was in a tent. Vaguely he was aware of the familiar sounds of a cavalry detachment: horses stamping at the lines, a noncom barking orders somewhere in the distance. He closed his eyes, slept once more. Next time a touch awakened him.

"Mr. Calhoon," a woman's voice said.

Calhoon opened his eyes, looked into the green ones of the girl of the corridor. His head ached only mildly now. With an effort he collected some of his faculties. "You—"

"Easy. I'm Evelyn Killraine. Your friends are here."

"Friends," Calhoon said.

"Mr. Whitton and Mr. Gannon." She straightened up, moved out of his range of vision. Dazedly, Calhoon was sorry to see her disappear. He tried to rise and find her again. Dizziness attacked him, but he stayed up, propped on his elbows.

"Loosh," said Henry Gannon's voice. "How you feel?"

The dizziness left Calhoon. Experimentally he turned his head, and though bandaged, it was all right now. Gannon and Whitton stood there by his bedside, looking at him with curiosity. The girl was with them, dressed now in blue, touches of white lace at her throat and sleeves.

"I'm all right, I reckon," Calhoon said and sat up. He knew a hospital tent when he saw one, although he seemed to be the only patient here. "Only, what—"

"Seems you had a run-in with Tod Isaacs again," Henry said dryly.

"Yeah," Calhoon said. Except for his boots, he was fully clothed. He looked around; the angle of light through canvas told him sunset was not far off.

"They say you worked him over pretty good, jest with one hand." Henry was grinning. "Only his bully boys grabbed you and pinned you, and he started in to gunwhip you. Likely he woulda killed you, except for Captain Killraine and this lady."

Calhoon looked at the girl inquiringly. He still could not quite believe how beautiful she was. It had been so long since he had seen such a woman—

She said with perfect composure, "You're very lucky, Mr. Calhoon. My brother and I were just going for a ride. We came out on the courthouse porch just in time to see the man Isaacs about to hit you with that gun. Before he could do it a second time, Phil stopped him."

"Stopped him how?" mumbled Calhoon.

"Phil's pretty direct." She smiled faintly. "He pulled his own revolver and told Isaacs to stop or he'd shoot him."

Calhoon rubbed his face. "I'm obliged to Captain Killraine," he said groggily. "And you, ma'am . . ."

Her smile was gone now. "Phil's not the kind to let a man be beaten to death in cold blood out on the street. He had that crowd dispersed and you brought here to the dispensary. The contract surgeon looked you over and said you'd be all right. While you were unconscious, you mentioned Mr. Gannon's name. So Phil sent a messenger out to his ranch . . ." She paused. "You mentioned Gordon Weymouth's, too."

Calhoon raised his head. "What did I say?"

"Nothing," she said, "that made me think you would want Judge Weymouth to take responsibility for you.

Since I was the only one that heard it, I won't repeat it, assuming it is your private affair."

So she was smart as well as lovely. Calhoon got unsteadily to his feet. "Then I'm doubly obliged," he said.

She only shrugged, then said, "Mr. Gannon and Mr. Whitton came straight in. They said they'd see to you."

"Loosh," Gannon said, "you'd better come back out to the ranch with us. Wherever it is you figure you got to ride, you're gonna need a day or two to get ironed out. And Double Oaks ain't the place to do it."

"No," Calhoon said. "I guess not." It all came back to him now, and he thought: *Washington* . . . He had to plan. But right now he was too weak, too drained. "Thanks, Henry." He looked around. "My boots . . ."

"Here." The girl produced them from under the foot of the cot. Still groggy, Calhoon sat on the bed and fumbled with them, cursing his one-handed awkwardness silently, aware of the girl's eyes on him. Then Evelyn Killraine said softly, "Let me help you." Before Calhoon could protest, she was beside him, and his nostrils were suddenly full of a clean, feminine fragrance; he could feel the warmth of her body close to his, and her arm brushed his thigh as she bent over him. Then he had the boots on, and she straightened up, brushing back a wisp of reddish-brown hair. "There."

"Again, thanks," Calhoon said. "I—" He broke off as Philip Killraine came through the tent's doorway and stopped. Killraine's eyes shuttled from Calhoon to his sister, then back again. "So you're up and about, Mr. Calhoon."

"We're fixin' to ride." Henry Gannon said.

"Not before I find out a little bit more about all this," Killraine said sharply. "You come into town seeking Gordon Weymouth. Then you wind up in a fight with Tod Isaacs on the very steps of the courthouse, even challenging him. Beat him, I might add, very badly and would have been gunwhipped to death perhaps yourself if I hadn't intervened. You stirred up a lot of dust in a very short time, Mr. Calhoon. I'll have more information about

you, if you please." His eyes went to Calhoon's gray pants.
"What outfit?"

"Captain," Calhoon replied instinctively. "South
Carolina Black Horse."

"Those," Killraine said tersely. "Yes. We've met them
on the field. I lost some good comrades to your troop,
Captain."

"I'm sorry," Calhoon said wearily. "Reckon it worked
both ways."

Killraine eased. "I suppose it did. That's in the past,
anyhow. All the same, the responsibility for peace and
order in this area rests on me and— You asked for Gordon Weymouth. I want to know what your business with
him is."

Calhoon sucked in a deep breath. "Private," he said.

"No," Killraine said. "I want an answer. When a former
Confederate captain, armed, comes here inquiring for a
former Union officer, I want to know what he's about."

"And I said it was private," Calhoon snapped.

"Phil—" Evelyn began, but Killraine motioned her to
silence. Short and stocky as he was, no older than Calhoon
himself, he reminded the South Carolinian somehow of the
emblem of his native state, the gamecock, small, compact,
bred to fight.

"Well, Captain," Killraine said, "I can't force you to
answer. But I have a feeling that for the sake of peace in
this county, the best thing for you to do is leave it—and I
mean immediately. I'm prepared to give you an escort or
travel in an ambulance to the county line. It is, sir, for
your safety as well as others. You handed Isaacs a beating,
and he's not a man to forget that. So unless you have legit-
imate business interests here, I'll have you out immediately."

"You mean you gonna roust him?" Henry Gannon
asked, voice crackling with anger.

"It's best for him and everyone. The doctor says he's fit
to travel, and I want him on his way."

"Phil, that's not fair!" Evelyn Killraine said angrily.

"I'll be the judge of that," Killraine answered. His voice
softened. "Ev, you know as well as I do that this town,

this whole district, is a powder keg. Something tells me this man is a spark that might— If he has no business here, I want him gone. I have trouble enough with Weymouth and Isaacs as it is."

"But he *got* business here," Elias Whitton cut in.

Calhoon and Killraine both looked at him. The black man took a step forward, blocky and thick in his brush-scarred leather. "He got real business here. Why, he own one-third of Rancho Bravo."

Henry Gannon jerked his head around, stared at Elias. Then he grinned. "Yeah," he said. "Yeah, that's so. You can't roust him, Killraine. He owns property."

"What property?" Killraine was frowning, baffled.

"A duly registered cattle brand in me and Elias Whitton's names. He's in on it, too, with a one-third interest. And since there are several hundred cattle wearin' that brand, he's a property owner, and you can't force him to leave."

Killraine shook his head. "You'll have to give me proof of that."

"You wait a minnit," Gannon said. He fumbled in his pocket, brought out a tiny notebook, searched until he found a stub of pencil. They all looked at him as, tongue protruding in concentration, he placed the book on one leather-clad knee and began to write. He finished with a flourish, passed the book to Whitton. "Sign that."

The tent was silent as Whitton, with apparent ease, read it, then wrote his name. Then he passed the notebook and pencil to Calhoon. "You write your'n at the bottom."

Calhoon read Gannon's scrawl. "This is to certify that one-third interest in the cattle brand RB, standing for Rancho Bravo, is hereby transferred to Lucius Calhoon for value received." Gannon's and Whitton's names followed, and then: "Receipt of above acknowledged." Gannon had drawn a line for Calhoon's signature.

Calhoon raised his head, looked at them. "I can't—" he began.

"Sign the durned thing," Gannon said. "We'll talk about it later. Cap'n Killraine, you can witness all these signatures."

Lucius Calhoon still hesitated. He did not, he thought, want any part of Rancho Bravo, touched as he was by this gesture. All he wanted was Gordon Weymouth . . . He gripped the pencil harder. But Gordon was in Washington, and he had no money or resources with which to follow h'm. Nevertheless . . . And then Calhoon saw it. *Yes,* he thought. *Here. This is the place he'll have to come back to sooner or later. And when he does, I'll be waiting . . .*

Decisively then, in bold dark script he signed his name. Then, grinning, he passed the book to Killraine.

Killraine read it, fingering his moustache. "C-a-l-h-o-o-n. I thought South Carolinians spelled it with a *u*."

"I'm not in South Carolina now," Calhoon said quietly. "I'm in Texas. And whatever happens to me here, I want certain people back home to be able to claim they never heard of me."

Killraine snorted. Shaking his head, he closed the book, passed it back to Gannon. "All right, you've outflanked me. All the same—"

Before he could go on, Whitton spoke up again. "You wanta know why he had a run-in with Isaacs? I tell you that much. You listen." Then, tersely he told Killraine what had happened the day before. "If it ain't for this man, I be swingin' from a limb right now. You talk about value received, that the value I got from him."

"Well, I'll be damned." Killraine's face turned dark. "You mean Isaacs tried to lynch you?"

"He wanted that buckskin of mine. Hadn't been for Loosh Calhoon, I be dead this minute."

"Phil," the girl said, looking at Calhoon strangely.

"Wait a minute," Killraine said. He rubbed his face thoughtfully. Then as if he had made up his mind to something, he dropped his hand. "All of you," he said. "I think all of you had better come over to my office right now."

Captain Philip Killraine's office in the courthouse was simply furnished: desk, a few chairs, and on the wall, an American flag, below it the regimental flag of the Seventh Cavalry and a troop guidon. There Calhoon, Henry, Elias, and Evelyn Killraine sat in the chairs he had gestured them to, looking silently at the Union officer as he paced back and forth, pulling at his moustache in that characteristic gesture.

Then Killraine halted, turned to face them. "Yes," he said, as if to himself. "Yes, I think that's what's indicated. Mr. Whitton!"

Elias sat up straight.

Killraine went to his desk, dropped into the chair behind it, took paper from a drawer, and a pen from an inkwell. "So Isaacs tried to murder you, eh? And three others of his men helping him?"

"I done told you that."

"Can you identify those other three?"

"They Ed Bodie, Sam Bickett, and one called, lemme see—yeah, I recollect his name. Will Tolliver."

"Ah, yes." Killraine grinned, exactly like a cat full of cream. "Then maybe you'd like to make a complaint to the military authorities—meaning me—against them for attempted murder."

"Huh?" Elias let out that one gasp. Otherwise, the room was silent.

"I said, if you complain to me, make charges against them, I shall then proceed to place them under military arrest and hold them pending instructions from General Sheridan in New Orleans and Colonel Granger in Galveston."

"Me?" Elias said. "Have 'em arrested?"

"Exactly." Now Killraine's voice was crisp, precise. "My orders," he said, "are to keep the peace in this county, carry out instructions of the federal Treasury agent, cooperate with the civil authorities as much as possible, and above all else, guarantee the life and liberty of freedmen like yourself. In short—" his eyes went from Gannon to Calhoon "—to keep the die-hards from abusing black people." Beneath his moustache, his lips curved faintly. "You, Mr. Whitton, are at present the only citizen in the United States in good standing among the three of you. Captain Calhoon and Mr. Gannon bore arms against the Republic, and their legal status is still unclear, whatever oaths they may have taken. There's no doubt about where you stand though, Mr. Whitton. You're one of the main reasons why we fought the war and why I'm here."

He shoved back his chair, arose, began to pace again as if too full of energy to sit for long. "I'll be frank with all of you. I'm waging an unequal struggle here. I'm ordered to keep the peace, I *mean* to keep the peace. But I've got only a handful of men to do it with, and Isaacs and his Regulators are the worst thorns in my side. Maybe you know Judge Weymouth and I have different views on things—"

Gannon growled, "Yeah. His view's to grab everything he can git his hands on."

"I'll neither agree with that nor dispute it. I'll only say that I did not fight this war in order to be used by politicians to settle their own private grudges and line their own pockets. I fought it in the hope that eventually bitterness can be erased and, as President Johnson and President Lincoln before him planned, the Confederate states can be brought back into the Union they had no right to leave. Meanwhile, here I am with a few troops, and there's Isaacs at the head of his own private army. It would mean a lot to peace and order here if Tod Isaacs and these other three—all key men—could be taken out of circulation for a while. If you'll sign a complaint, Mr. Whitton, I'll see that's done." He smiled faintly. "My authority allows me to hold them without bond in such a matter."

"And Weymouth cain't get 'em loose?" Whitton asked wonderingly.

"Not until they either stand trial or General Sheridan orders some other disposition of the case."

"Judas Priest," Gannon whispered. "That would git Isaacs off our necks for . . . how long?"

"Weeks at least," Killraine said.

"And Weymouth'll blow up like a powder house!" Gannon blurted.

"This is a matter outside of Judge Weymouth's jurisdiction. Well, Mr. Whitton?"

Elias still seemed thunderstruck. Then his mouth closed with a snap. "If it take Tod Isaacs off our back, you jest show me what to sign!"

"The papers will be ready in a minute." Killraine turned to Evelyn. "Sis, will you sit here at my desk and write what I dictate?"

Evelyn Killraine arose, smiling. "Nothing would make me happier," she said.

Elias Whitton laid aside the pen, stood up. "There," he said. "That all there is to it, Cap'n?"

"That's all," Killraine said. He picked up the papers and looked at them with satisfaction. "This will make my job infinitely easier. Thank you, Mr. Whitton."

"When you goan pick up Isaacs?" Elias asked.

"I'll issue orders directly."

"Captain," Gannon said, also arising, "I thank—"

Killraine's head snapped up. "Spare me your thanks, Mr. Gannon. This was not done for your benefit or for Captain Calhoon's or to settle any private grudge of mine. This was merely in accordance with my orders, which, sir, I assure you I will follow to the letter without favoritism."

His voice rang with sincerity. Lucius Calhoon, who had sat unmoving all this time, looked at Killraine with the admiration of one seasoned officer for another, knowing the little captain meant it. He waited a moment longer before also arising. During the fifteen minutes it had taken for Killraine to dictate the necessary papers, questioning Whitton as he did so, Calhoon had remained entirely silent. But the South Carolinian's mind, clear now, had been working. He had sized up Killraine, and he had done more than that. He had sized up Rancho Bravo, too, and he knew now what it meant to him. Gordon Weymouth was out of reach, but Joshua Weymouth was still here. *And,* Calhoon thought, *hurt the father bad enough and the son will have to come back.*

And so now he saw clearly how he just might do it. The scribbled document giving him one-third interest in Rancho Bravo; the color of Elias Whitton's skin; those men on the porches of the saloons, waiting, as Henry had said, for something to happen but not knowing what. And he had remembered, too, an old maxim of Jeb Stuart's and Hampton's: the doctrine of the cavalry. *First know your ground, then charge the bastards!* And now, he thought, he knew the ground.

So he stood up. "One more thing, Captain."

Killraine turned, brows arching. "Sir?"

"Mr. Whitton here—" Calhoon jerked his thumb "—has already been the object of one attempted murder while carrying out his business. Even with Isaacs and the others in custody, his life may still be in danger. So Mr. Whitton requests, sir, as a United States citizen, protection from the US Army."

For a moment the room was silent. Then Killraine said, blinking, "He has that, sir."

"Not the way he needs it. What he needs is a detail assigned to him permanently, to protect him while he goes about his business."

"A detail—" Killraine's face reddened. "You mean an escort out of town? All right, that's reasonable."

"I mean an escort in town while we go about certain business and a permanent detail to protect Mr. Whitton's life and property for an indefinite length of time."

"Captain Calhoon—" Killraine's face turned a deeper red.

"Elias Whitton, sir," Calhoon went on precisely, "is engaged in the cattle business as one-third owner of the Rancho Bravo brand. Right now he's rounding up a herd and getting it ready to make a drive to market. There are certain interests in this county, so I understand, who might use force to prevent that. It seems reasonable that as a freedman, a citizen of the United States, and a businessman, that Mr. Whitton would be entitled to a permanent detail of soldiers to guard both him and his herd. It wouldn't have to be many, just two or three. So long as it was understood, of course, that any interference with Mr. Whitton or attack on those soldiers would be dealt with sternly and with force by your entire command."

Philip Killraine's mouth opened and closed like a stranded fish's. Then he recovered and smiled. "Oh, I see, Captain. You think you can use Elias Whitton—"

"Leaving aside the fact that you just did," Calhoon said, "suppose Mr. Whitton asks you for such protection himself. Then, of course, it's up to you to decide whether or not it's within your orders to provide it." He turned his head. "Elias?"

Whitton had grasped it now, and he was grinning broadly. "Hell, yes!" he said and then apologized to the girl. "I mean, sho, Captain. Even with Isaacs locked up, Weymouth still got plenty Regulators left! But not even he dare mess with us if American soldiers there and he draw down the lightnin' on him by shootin' or botherin' 'em!" He laughed richly. "You want to keep the peace, no better way than you give us a few of yo' cavalrymen to watch our herd. I mean, my herd, my property. Yeah, I request that. I request that officially."

"Why—" Killraine tugged furiously at his moustache.

Then the girl's soft laughter broke the silence. "Phil. They've got you boxed in. You can't deny Mr. Whitton that protection when they've tried to murder him once already."

Killraine only stood there for a moment. Then he dropped his hand, and his face changed. Now it was absolutely expressionless. "You think there's a real threat to your life, Mr. Whitton?"

Elias was dead serious now. "I know doggone well there is. We aim to round up as many cattle offa Gannon's land as we can, and Weymouth don't wanna see 'em go. Isaacs or no, he have men out there to stampede our herd, maybe bushwhack us, and blow us outa the saddle unless you give us soldiers. I mean, you don't think he'll take Isaacs gittin' whupped and then arrested lyin' down? And you know how he feels about Henry Gannon." His eyes were hard. "Yeah. Without them troopers he come after us. And then he either kill us, or we gotta kill some people our ownselves."

"Umm . . ." Then, quite unexpectedly, Killraine grinned. "Very well. Request granted. I'll put a detail of three men at your disposal, with orders to guard your person, Mr. Whitton, yours alone—you understand?—and

your property. The initial assignment's for one week; at
the end of that time I'll decide whether to keep them there
or withdraw them, depending on how things look. And I'll
make sure everyone knows that an attack on you is an attack on the United States Army and will be dealt with ac-
cordingly." His grin went away as he looked at Calhoon.
"But you," he said. "I haven't forgot who you asked for in
this courthouse. And until I know why you wanted him,
you had better walk a chalk line. You're smart, Calhoon.
Make sure you're not too smart for your own good. Because if you break the peace, I'll give you the same treatment I'm giving Isaacs—and you might find me even
rougher to deal with."

Calhoon said nothing, and the captain turned away.
"I'll give orders for the detail to come up. It should be
here in fifteen minutes; meanwhile . . . Evelyn, it's almost
sundown. I think you'd better go on home. I don't want
you on the streets of this place after dark."

The girl arose. "Yes, Phil, I'll start supper." She looked
at the three of them. "Mr. Gannon, Mr. Whitton, Captain
Calhoon—" Her eyes met Calhoon's. "I wish you luck.
Good night, gentlemen." She hesitated, still looking at
Calhoon, then turned, and went out.

When she was gone, Killraine said, "The three of you
wait here a minute while I give instructions to my order-
ly." He followed his sister through the door from his inner
office to an outer one.

When they had gone, Gannon said gustily, "Well, I be
damned. Loosh, you sure ran a whizzer—" There was admiration in his eyes.

"Never mind that," Calhoon cut him off. "Henry, listen.
How does a man register a brand in this county?"

"Why—" Gannon blinked. "He jest walks in the registration office across the hall and registers it, that's all."

"There's no fee?"

"Nothing. Don't cost a penny. Anybody can do it, long
as he's of age." He frowned. "Loosh, what you driving
at?"

"Because," Calhoon said, "with those soldiers we can

keep Weymouth off our neck while we hire some riders to-night."

Henry's jaw dropped. "Hire? Loosh, I done told you—"

"I know what you told me." Calhoon spoke rapidly, wanting to get it all out while Killraine was gone. "But I saw those men today, sittin' out there on the porches of the saloons, just waitin' to go to work—"

"For wages—"

"What are wages?"

"Anything they can git. A quarter a day on up."

"Wouldn't a cow be worth a quarter?"

Gannon and Whitton looked at one another.

"Because you got to face it," Calhoon went on. "The three of us can't do it by ourselves. Not two thousand head in three months. We've got to have help. Now answer my question, what's a longhorn worth on the hoof?"

"I told you, not a damn thing, everybody's cattle poor—"

"Henry," Calhoon said patiently, "you're thinkin' like a man with five or six thousand herd. Try thinkin' like one that doesn't own a single cow to his name—or anything else that he can call his own."

"Wait a minute," Elias said. "Wait, I think I see—"

"Why not?" Calhoon asked. "All those men in Double Oaks who want to work? Suppose each registers a brand in his own name? Then for every Rancho Bravo cow he brings in, he can put his own brand on another. If he brings in two head of Rancho Bravo stock a day, he's got two head of his own. If twenty men went for that and you figure ninety days, that's forty head a day for us, more than three thousand head before your deadline hits, and every rider that goes along with that, he'd have nearly two hundred of his own. You give a man two hundred head of cattle when he's flat broke, I'll bet you he'd fight Weymouth or anybody else and work himself to skin and bones in the bargain!"

When Calhoon broke off, there was only silence. Then Whitton said tensely, "Henry—"

But Gannon was dropping into a chair, almost limply. "Well, I'll be goddamned," he whispered. "I'll just be—Loosh."

"You think it'd work?"

"Work?" Now Henry sat up straight. "Hell, yes, it'd work. All we got to do is go from bar to bar and spread the word, and soldiers at our back so we don't hafta fight while we're doin' it—" Suddenly he threw back his head and laughed, a crashing laugh almost hysterical, full of breaking tension. And Whitton's grin grew broader. "Oh, hell," Gannon said, "it's so simple now. It's so dadblame simple! Why didn't I think of that a long time ago?" He jumped to his feet. All at once his ugly face was sober, hard again, but his eyes gleamed with a light that was fantastic. "Twenty riders, thirty, we can comb that range and stand off anything Josh Weymouth can throw against us! Pick it clean as a whistle, not leave a single cow for that bastard to get his hands on! Let him take that brush! By the time he does, we'll be on our way to the promised land!" He thrust out his left hand. "Loosh," he said more quietly, "welcome to Rancho Bravo!"

Calhoon gripped Henry's with his own. But even as he shook it, he felt guilty. Rancho Bravo was Henry Gannon's dream. If he thought Calhoon shared it, he was wrong. Calhoon's dream was wholly different, but he could use Henry's bright one to make his own bitter one come true.

Chapter 6

Calhoon had made his scout; and now he returned to the clearing just in time to see it happen. Out of the brush they came: five longhorns, heads down and tails curled high; and then they saw the riders waiting for them.

Three old cows, a yearling, and a huge black bull with forward-pointing horns like sabers, they sheered off as they saw the men and, bellowing, tried to dodge back in the thicket. But more riders smashed through the chaparral behind them, and the cattle broke and ran down the long stretch of prairie. Letting out a shrill, gobbling yell, a Comanche war cry, Elias Whitton spurred his horse and swung his loop. Henry Gannon cut loose with a scream of the kind the South Carolinian had heard in many a charge, a Rebel yell, and took off in pursuit, too, and hoofs thundered as the other four riders in the clearing joined the chase. Calhoon watched Gannon with admiration because Henry was a genius at this sort of thing and with envy because Gannon had two good hands. While the others went after the cows, Henry rode down the bull. As if it had a life of its own, his rawhide loop reached out, cleared the wide horns, closed around the brute's neck. Then Gannon's wiry mustang skidded to a halt, braced itself, and a thousand pounds of bull hit the *riata*'s end at full speed.

The impact jerked horse and rider both, as the tie around the saddle horn and double cinches took the strain. The bull was jerked off its feet, landed hard, and Henry was just jumping free of the saddle, the *peal,* the tie-rope, in his hands, when Calhoon yelled.

But Henry saw it, too, the great black animal already scrambling to its feet. With one foot stirrupless he came back down on the horse, and then the bull was charging up the rope, huge and black, its bellow as loud and chilling as the blast of a runaway locomotive.

There was no time for Gannon to act, the horse took control, knowing its business as thoroughly as its rider. As the bull bore down on it, the horse dodged and reared, and in a tangle of rawhide the huge creature, hooking viciously, slammed on by, horn just missing the mustang's chest. Then again it hit rope's end, and this time the impact flipped it over in a somersault. It hit on its spine, so hard it seemed to jar the earth, and lay there breathless. Before it could move, the little horse had put a strain on the rope again and Gannon, the *peal* between his teeth, was out of the saddle and running. His hands flew as he bent over the great animal, and he got the two hind feet tied before it tried to scramble up on its front ones. Henry dodged slashing horns, jumped back, and the horse pulled the rope tight once more and dragged the bull's head down, and then Henry finished his tie. Panting, face triumphant, he looked around. Four more animals, hogtied like the bull, lay here and there around the clearing, and Elias was already gathering wood for a branding fire. Henry's exultant shout rang above the bellowing: "Five more for Rancho Bravo!"

Five more for Rancho Bravo! Calhoon himself felt a wild triumph as he loped on into the clearing, where now Gannon, Elias, and six lean young Texas brushpoppers were wiping sweat from their faces and picking thorns from themselves and their horses, or coiling ropes. Like them Calhoon was clad now in brush clothes: flannel shirt, leather jacket, leather leggings, the Confederate hat anchored with a rawhide chinstrap. This was gear that had belonged to Henry's dead brother; it was not the first time in the past five years that Calhoon had worn a dead man's clothes.

Gannon saw him coming, strode forward to meet him with a wide grin on his rough-hewn face. "Loosh, how is it? All quiet?"

"So far," Calhoon said.

"Good." Henry gestured. "Five more." He took out his

little pocket notebook, thumbed through it, made a jot with the pencil. "Three weeks," he said, "and we've gathered near six hundred head for Rancho Bravo. With what me and Elias already had, that puts us just about halfway there. We'll brand these and tie 'em out to simmer down. Think I'll cut that bull. That'll about clean up this thicket. Then we'll bring in the ones we tied out yesterday. Tomorrow, I think we'll move over to the Old Stump thicket and start to work that."

"Right," Calhoon said. "Go on with your work. I'll cover you."

"Yeah," Henry said. "You keep your eyes open. And for God's sake, Loosh, don't git so busy watchin' our backs you forget about your own."

Calhoon grinned, swung his Morgan. Then once more he set off on scout.

Three weeks. A lot, Lucius Calhoon thought as he rode slowly along a main trail through the brush, had happened in that time. In these three weeks he had watched Rancho Bravo grow from an impossible dream to hard reality, and he could not help a surge of pride in the part he himself had played in that.

His mind went back to that night in Double Oaks when Captain Killraine had returned with a corporal and two men. "Your orders," he told them, "are to protect Mr. Whitton here as he goes about his business, whatever that business may be, and his property as well. You'll carry out any lawful request he makes of you, and if you come under attack from any quarter, you are to return fire and shoot to kill. Your supplies will be brought to the Gannon ranch in the morning, and you'll either be relieved or re-supplied there in one week. Is that clear?"

Neither the noncom nor the troopers looked happy about those orders, but the corporal's salute was smart.

"Carry on," Killraine said and turned to the three. "Gentlemen, I bid you good day. A detail's already been sent out to arrest Isaacs and the other three. And . . ." He slapped his gauntlets against his palm. "Let me issue a warning to all of you. I've offered you protection against

violence. I assure you that if you yourself start any violence, that protection will not only be withdrawn, but I'll
snap you up just as quickly as I'm taking Isaacs. Do I
make myself clear?"

"Very clear," Calhoon said.

"Then goodnight." He turned away.

"Come on," Whitton said to the soldiers. "We still got
business here in town, and you three better stick to us
tight as ticks to a calf's hocks."

When they left Killraine's office, the other offices in the
courthouse were closed. It was growing dark as they went
out on the street. "Loosh," Henry Gannon said, "your
guns seems to have got lost in the shuffle." He drew one of
his own Starr revolvers and held it out. "Better tote this
for a while."

Calhoon nodded, holstered it. His Morgan was still at
the rack with the mounts of the other two and the horses
of the three cavalrymen. All of them swung up. Gannon
slapped his thigh. "Okay, gentlemen. Let's go and see if
we can round ourselves up a cow crowd."

In the twilight the cavalcade rode down the street, two
soldiers on its flanks, one trailing; and it made a spectacle
that caused men to turn and stare: a black man, a man in
Confederate hat and pants with a bandage on his head and
strips of cornplaster on his face, and Henry Gannon, obviously Texan through and through, escorted by troopers
of the United States. Calhoon grinned tightly to himself,
despite the aches each pace of the walking horse sent
through his battered person. If Joshua Weymouth were
witness to this, it would give him something to think
about.

Then Gannon pulled up at the first saloon. It was going
full blast, brightly lit and with the tinkle of a hurdy-gurdy
emanating from inside, but the porch was still full of men,
that same leathery breed of veteran exsoldiers without the
money to go inside and drink. "Loosh, 'Lias," Henry said.
"You and them troopers keep your eyes peeled." He
swung down, mounted the porch. Most of the men he
seemed to know, calling their names. "Doug; hello, Wes-
ley; howdy, Webb . . ."

They made room for him. "Hello, Henry . . ."

Gannon stood there among them, legs widespread, thumbs hooked in his belt. He looked at them a moment, the light from within playing over his hard features. Then his voice rang out. "All right, you brushpoppers! You've sat on your tails long enough! I need maverickers, all I can git, and I can't pay cash, but if you can use a rope and runnin' iron, by God, I can set you up in business for yourself!"

That seized their attention, and they gathered around. "Henry," one drawled, "what the hell you talkin' 'bout?"

"I'm talkin' about Rancho Bravo!" His voice soared. "I'm talkin' about a place way to hell and gone across the Pecos, where there's miles and miles of prime grass and no brush to chew you up, no goddamn Yankees to look down on you, and I'm talkin about miners in Colorado ready to pour a man's hands full of gold at the sight of a Texas cow! I got five, six thousand mavericks out there on my range, and I got to have at least two thousand in my own iron! Any man who wants to work, he's got this deal: come cow-huntin' with me in the shinnery and every beef you brand for Rancho Bravo, you strike your own iron on another. And if in ninety days ever' man jack of you don't own a herd of better than a hundred head under his own brand, he's been doggin' it!"

Their eyes lit at that, and they crowded in; and then the questions came. Gannon threw the answers back, deep voiced and confident. "Hell, all you got to do is walk down to the courthouse tomorrow mornin' and register yourself an iron. Isaacs? He won't bother us for a while. This cow hunt's under the protection of Yankee soldiers, you see? That don't mean you won't have to fight—but, hell, you've fought before!"

That hooked them—but not all of them. They looked at Elias Whitton, and the bitter question came. Henry answered it with harsh straightforwardness. "Now this you all got to understand. Elias is as much a ramrod in this as me or Loosh Calhoon from South Carolina, yonder. Without Elias there ain't no drive, there ain't no grass, there ain't no Rancho Bravo! So when he gives an order, it's to

be obeyed. You don't want to work that way, build your
own herd, start a new life, you'd rather spend the rest of
the summer broke and loafin' on this porch, suit yourself!
But it's Elias who'll take us to new range, Elias who'll deal
with the Comanches, and we can't do without him, and
neither can you. Me, I rode with Hood, like most of y'all,
and I'll tell you now, I'm proud to ride with Elias, too!"
His voice crackled. "As far as I'm concerned, the past is
dead. What I aim to have is a future, and when I die,
somethin' to pass on to my wife and kids, if I ever have any,
so they can say: Henry Gannon built this! Somethin' that
a hundred years from now will still be there and people
can look at it and know: Henry Gannon passed this way!
And the kind of men I want feel like that and would ride
with Satan himself to pull themselves out of the bog. The
others that don't, I say the hell with them anyhow!"

But the ancient prejudice ran deep in all of them, and
Calhoon, knowing it well himself, recognized it when it
surfaced. He was not surprised when most of them merely
spat and turned away. And yet . . . A third, perhaps,
looked thoughtful, hesitant, tempted.

"Y'all know where my home ranch is," Gannon finished. "Anybody that wants to set hisself up in business
with my beef, register a brand and be there come noon tomorrow. You'll live hard, off of beef and branch water
and not much else, and you won't have two four-bit pieces
to rub together in your pockets for a long, long time. But,
by God, you'll own a brand and cattle with it on their
ribs!"

There was silence. Gannon looked from face to face.
"All right," he said. "You think about it. Noon tomorrow
at my ranch." Then he turned, jumped off the porch,
picked up his horse's reins, and walked to the bar across
the street to begin his spiel all over again.

And so it went up and down the street. The reception
was almost identical everywhere, and Elias Whitton's
mouth tightened in a thin line. "Look like I the dead dog
in the spring in this operation . . ."

"They'll come," Gannon said. "Don't you worry, 'Lias.

Not all of 'em, no. But the hungry ones and the smart ones. They'll come, and we'll have our cow crowd." He grinned and clapped Whitton on the back. "Anyhow, it ain't the sight of you, it's all these Yankee uniforms." Mounted now, he reined his horse around. "Well, we've worked 'em all except The Texas Flag, and I don't expect many of Isaacs' men would care to jine us. So we'll head on home. It's been a right full day."

They rode out into the street. Then Whitton said tensely, "Hold up. Look a-yonder." He pointed toward The Texas Flag and as he did so, a voice rang out, deep and angry: "Gannon!"

Calhoon sat straight up in the saddle as he saw the tall figure, silhouetted against the yellow light pouring from the saloon. The man came down the steps, strode toward them across the street. There was something familiar in that walk, in the man's carriage. And then, with a tightening in his throat he knew; and instinctively his hand went to the butt of his revolver.

Light from the saloon they'd just left fell on the man as he planted himself squarely before their horses. Calhoon saw, beneath the black slouch hat, the mane of iron-gray hair, the head of curious shape, wide at the eyes, pointed of nose and chin and strangely wolfish in appearance. It was the same, exactly the same. He seemed to feel agony again where a right hand that did not exist should be, as he stared at Joshua Weymouth.

Weymouth, wearing a frock coat, white shirt with collar and string tie, striped pants, and shoes, looked back at him for a long moment, as if fixing Calhoon in his mind. Then he turned his gaze to Elias Whitton.

"Mr. Whitton," he said tautly, "I'd like to talk to you."

"Why, Jedge Weymouth," Whitton said, "you go ahead and talk."

"Privately."

"These men my partners. Anything you wanta say you say in fronta them. Maybe you ain't met Loosh Calhoon. Loosh, Judge Josh Weymouth."

"I know about Calhoon," Weymouth said harshly; and

the South Carolinian tensed. Then the judge went on,
"He's the one who fought with Isaacs. But it's you my business is with. I insist you give me some time—"

Elias laughed softly. "Say it here, Jedge."

Weymouth's face worked. Then he nodded. "Very well.
Mr. Whitton, you're in with the wrong crowd. I simply
can't understand how a man like you could let himself be
used by men like these two. Don't you realize, sir, that
these men fought to hold you in slavery?"

"Nobody hold me in slavery," Whitton said. "I free myself. Long time ago."

"These men are your enemies. They're just using you!
So is, I'm sorry to say, Captain Killraine, to work off his
personal grudge against me."

"Jedge, what you drivin' at?" Elias asked.

Weymouth said, "You've sworn out warrants against
Tod Isaacs and three other men. Gannon has used you to
procure soldiers to protect his own skin. But what do you
think you're going to get out of all this? Why should a man
of your character throw in with people like these?" He
lowered his voice a little. "Mr. Whitton, if we could only
talk in private a few minutes. The Republican Party and
the Loyal League could use a man like you—"

Whitton only looked at him with wry amusement.
"Jedge, where the Party and Loyal League at yestiddy
when Isaacs and his men try to hang me?"

"That was a misunderstanding—"

"And a damned nigh fatal one." Suddenly Whitton's
voice went hard. "You think I don't appreciate it?" he
said. "You think I don't appreciate all the things them
Federal soldiers did for the sake of me and my kind? A
man like Killraine, I put my hand in the fire for him. But a
man like you—" Whitton's voice was withering with contempt. "You and Isaacs. Buzzards, that all. Jest buzzards
come down to feed on a dead carcass, gobble all the rotten
meat you kin hold." He spat in the dust. "What yo' Party
and the Loyal League gonna offer me? Chance to betray
my friends, be a buzzard, too, link up with people tried to
kill me? How much you gonna pay me to withdraw them

warrants, whut you gonna offer?" He rose in his stirrups. "How you goan match what I already got—freedom to ride the country, work at what I know, risk my neck to build myself a fortune out beyond the Pecos? Whut you goan give me in place of that—some high-soundin' title and a town hat to wear and shoes?" He spat again. "When you got a thousand miles of free grass and a herd of feisty longhawns strung out from can to can't and the wind blowin' free agin' my face to offer me, maybe then you and me talk business. Until then you want niggers, you go find some tame ones. Let this hawse alone. Now. Be kind enough to git out of our road."

Weymouth's face worked some more, thin lips twitching. "You are insolent, sir."

"No," Whitton said. "Jest busy. We got to ride. Stand clear. Come mornin', we got cattle to round up."

Weymouth did not move. "All right," he said after a moment. "So be it; if you want to throw in with the enemy, you'll have to be treated as an enemy."

Whitton let out a gusty breath. "Last time I heard, the war was over, and there weren't no more enemies. But, Jedge, I'll tell you this—" He turned in his saddle, pointed. "You see these here men in uniform? They ain't my soldiers, they are *yours*. They are givin' me the pertection you talk so big about. So if you come at me, you are comin' at your own people. You think about that and talk about it with Killraine. Now, like I said, will you stand clear? We got a long ride to make before we lay down to sleep tonight."

Another silent moment; then Weymouth rigidly stepped aside. "Gannon—"

Henry looked at him.

"Less than ninety days. You'd better damn well have the money or be clear of that range by then."

"We'll be clear. In fact, Judge, there won't be a cow left on it when we leave if I can help it. Meantime, though, that's still my land. If I were you, I'd pass the word. Anybody trespassin' on it may go out weighin' a lot more than he did when he come in, and the difference is likely

to be more lead than he can tote. Goodnight, Judge."
Gannon touched his hat, spurred his horse into a run. As
Weymouth jumped back, the others followed.

As they galloped down the street, Calhoon twisted in
the saddle. The tall man stood there in the center of the
street, staring after them. At the sight of that gaunt silhouette, Calhoon thought again: *Hurt the father bad enough
and the son'll come to him.* He swung forward and rode
on with the night wind in his face.

As he circled warily through the brush, Lucius Calhoon
put the memory of the night from him and concentrated
on what lay at hand. With his Henry rifle across the saddle, he rode slowly, eyes searching the shinnery, as Gannon called it, and the trail ahead. Sometimes he stopped
and looked up at the sky. The movement of birds could be
as much a part of reading signs as looking for hoofprints
or campfire smoke or embers . . .

But the sea of brush, the great *brasada,* lay awesome
and seemingly empty before him, under a sky of flawless
blue, great thicket after thicket, separated one from the
other by grassy prairies or clumps of forest. To Calhoon it
was still a strange, exotic, and fascinating kind of country.
Again he thought of the wild swamps at home along the
Wateree and Santee Rivers, places so thick and secret and
hidden that there were still miles of them that, after more
than a century, no white man had ever penetrated. The
brasada, the ocean of brush stretching from the Nueces,
they said, to the Rio Grande, was like that, only lacking
the giant trees but on an even more grandiose scale. Even
now his mind still had to wrestle with the hugeness and
freshness and grandeur of Texas. This country was big
and wild enough; what must it be like beyond the Pecos?
He could not imagine, having only Elias Whitton's de-
scriptions to go on.

And they were staggering in their dimensions, though
Elias could not always find the words he sought. Maybe
there were no words for the hugeness of the sky and of the
land, the great herds of buffalo, the wild tribes that fed on
them, the almost-as-wild Mexican Comancheros who

came up from the south to hunt and trade. Yet, somehow, it was all vivid in Calhoon's mind: the great tableland above the Big Bend of the Rio, the Staked Plain beyond, and the shining mountains north and west. The southeast, he thought, Virginia, the Carolinas, Georgia: he had fought over all of them, and they were like ravished women, tired of resisting and drained of youth. But Texas, by God, was still a virgin, young, lusty, strong, waiting defiantly for the man powerful enough to conquer and overcome her and force her to surrender . . .

But for now it was the brush he dealt with, and he did it meticulously. It was his task to course through it like a hound, sniffing and nosing at everything. It took two good hands to hunt and tie wild cattle plus much experience that he lacked. But he had plenty of experience at fighting and could do it with one hand, so while the men of Rancho Bravo worked, it was his task to stay out on their flanks and guard them against any ambush Weymouth might set up.

That assignment had been given to him the day following the one in town. When they had reached Gannon's ranch, Elias, with the three soldiers, had ridden off to guard the pens where the cattle Whitton and Henry had already gathered were held. Gannon and Calhoon had remained behind in the ranch house, waiting, Calhoon meanwhile fitting himself out in the clothes of Gannon's dead brother.

"You think they'll come?" Calhoon asked, fastening big-roweled spurs on his boots.

Gannon stood at the window, watching the sandy road. "They'll come," he said with confidence. "Some of 'em. We put that proposition to a hundred men. Sho'ly twenty of 'em, anyhow, will jump at it . . ."

"We'd have had a hundred then and there if it hadn't been for Elias," Calhoon said.

Henry turned. "That gall you, too?"

Calhoon fastened the strap, stood up. "It did at first. Not all that much now. A black woman helped raise me; I played with a black boy; a black body servant went off to war with me—I sent him home because it was too danger-

ous. He had too much guts, kept riding into trouble along
with me and him not armed, wouldn't stay behind. When I
came home from the war, yeah, and they had all gone off,
it was like they had . . . deserted me. But— I don't know.
It's damned complicated. All I know is this: I hate losing
everything they cost me, including this hand; but this is a
new country and a new time, and Elias Whitton is a lot of
man. I'll get along with him."

"You'll have to," Gannon said. "Because—" Then he
broke off. "Loosh—"

But Calhoon had already heard it, too. New spurs jingling, he followed Gannon through the front door and off
the porch into the heat of a sun nearing zenith.

Down the sandy road, around a bend, the thunder of
hoofbeats grew louder. Then they swept into sight, riding
at a lope, the men in leather or Confederate gray, all wearing guns and some leading extra horses.

Henry's voice was a crow of triumph. "You see? I told
you they'd be here—"

Calhoon did not answer. He was counting. Ten, fifteen,
twenty, twenty-two . . . Among them he saw Mexicans
with coffee skins and at least one black. They pounded
into the ranch yard, and a tall one with a face like a blade
tipped back his battered hat and danced his mustang out
in front. "Howdy, Henry."

"Wes . . . I see you've come."

"We've come. We thought about what you said. And
this many of us, anyhow, we're tired of bein' busted. A
man without no money or no property ain't no man at all.
So we went down to the courthouse and registered our
brands. If you meant that about one cow each for ever'
Rancho Bravo beef we brand, we're here to take you up
on it."

"It was gospel," Henry said, eyes glowing, voice vi-
brant. "Any more comin' behind you?"

"Maybe later. There's a lot didn't like the idea of workin' for a nigger, more that didn't mind that but didn't like
bein' beholden to Yankee soldiers for protection. We all
know the situation, Henry. We know Josh Weymouth
won't take kindly to us takin' up cattle off this range as

well as you. But that don't make a damn. Me for one and the others feel the same way. Time I have my iron on a single yearlin', I'm ready to fight hell and all its devils to hold onto my property."

"And you may well have to." But Gannon was laughing with excitement. Then he turned. "Look here," he said. "I want you all to meet Loosh Calhoon. He's the new partner, one-third interest in Rancho Bravo. He's from the East, but he's a cavalryman and a fighter, even if he's lost one hand. Captain, South Ca'lina Black Horse . . ."

A murmur arose from some of them. The man named Wes said, "I'm proud to know you, Captain Calhoon."

"Likewise," Calhoon said loudly. "All of you."

Henry Gannon said, "Now, y'all hear me. The way I got it figured is this: it'll take a while to make a cowman outa Loosh. But I know for a fact he don't need no more trainin' to use a gun. Besides, he's a planter, eddicated. Me, I ramrod this cow hunt. 'Lias Whitton is my straw-boss, and anybody don't like it can turn and go right now. Loosh Calhoon's job is this: he covers us, and he keeps the records."

He turned to Calhoon. "Isaacs' is on ice. But there are plenty more of his Regulators. When we start poppin' brush and diggin' cattle out, we ain't got time to watch for bushwhackers. I figure it will be up to you to protect us. You post those Yankee guards where you think they're needed, you take as many men as you figure you have got to have to help you, and you beat the brush around us for anybody who might be layin' up to do us a meanness while we work. We'll hunt cows all day and guard 'em at night; you hunt Regulators. Maybe you've got the toughest job. Okay?"

Calhoon felt a certain relief. He had been wondering what possible use a one-handed greenhorn could be to the Rancho Bravo cow hunt. But these were jobs he could do and, he knew, jobs that had to be done, were of crucial importance. He said immediately, "Right."

"Then all you fellers line up and let Loosh git your name and brand on a tally sheet. We got to have a record of every one, to treat you fair. And soon as he does that, we head out into the thickets. We got a powerful lot of work to do and damn little time left to do it in!"

So that was how Calhoon had become tally-keeper and chief guard on the cow hunt. And, he thought now, reining in the Morgan and leaning out of the saddle to examine a line of hoof prints across the clearing, if he had thought Henry Gannon was only making work for him, he had another think a-coming. Never in his life had he worked so hard.

He straightened up in the saddle, looked around the clearing, saw nothing to alarm him, then rode on, following the trail of a running horse, clearly gouged in the prairie. It had been made yesterday, he judged, and after years of hunting in South Carolina, he was expert at such matters; it was just a matter of adapting knowledge to new terrain. Presently he was satisfied that it offered no threat, made by one of the Texans.

Calhoon touched his shirt pocket. It held tobacco and cigarette papers, part of the rations Killraine had sent out, which the soldiers had shared with the men of Rancho Bravo. The first supply wagon had been lavish, far more than three men could consume. The bearded teamster had told the corporal, "Cap'n says he don't mind you share the leftovers with these people, but you charge 'em fer it, he'll have your butt." Tobacco, coffee, flour, beans; it had been a treasure trove for the bankrupt cowmen. That lavishness had puzzled some of them, but not Calhoon. It was, he knew, a gesture of compassion to the defeated enemy by the victor; and if he'd been in Killraine's boots, he'd have done the same. Grant had, in letting Lee's army keep its guns and horses.

Anyhow, the smoke tasted good as he sat on the horse in the shade of a mesquite. He let it dribble through his nostrils, thinking that presently he would start for the South Springs Pens, scout those, and the trail back to the Nine-Mile Thicket. South Springs, Nine-Mile, Old Stump . . . he was learning the country, soaking up the features of the terrain with the swiftness of the trained cavalryman. He could pretty well find his way around Gannon's enormous ranch now. He had learned a lot about Texas cattle, too.

Calhoon grinned. On the big plantation in South Carolina they had raised stock, too; and he'd helped round up cattle or hogs left to graze wild for the summer in the woods and swamps. That had been exciting, but nothing like this. It took a Texan born and bred to know how to handle longhorns, which were a breed all by themselves.

To an Eastern stockman, the damned things looked ridiculous, Calhoon thought. All horn and head and hips and hocks and great splayed hoofs and damned little beef in between. A breeder in South Carolina would have shot their kind on sight to keep them from contaminating his herd.

But they were ideally suited to this country. Those long horns could fight off wolves and coyotes, panthers and even jaguars; those tails that sometimes dragged the ground fought myriad insects, including the dreadful screwflies; those lanky frames could, in time of drought, live off the water stored in cactus. Like everything else in Texas they were built to weather hard times, and most had an immunity to the fever which the ticks infesting them spread to northern cattle. Unhorse a man, put him on foot among them, and they were as dangerous as so many Yankee cavalrymen. Even mounted, you had better be wary of the unexpected charge from some proddy, feisty bull or cow protecting her calf. God help you if you were slow tying one when it was down or your saddle cinches broke or your horse went over when your rope went tight. These were no gentle, lowing kine; these were, when they chose to be, killers.

So the Texans were rough with them, even brutal. One by one they chivied them out of brush, roped, tied, branded, and earmarked them. But it was impossible to drive them to the pens or herdbreak them until they'd been tamed. Usually they were tied to a tree, left to weaken from thirst and starvation until comparatively docile, then penned up until they got used to staying with a bunch,

after which they were thrown into the big herd held by
riders on the open prairie. But the toughest ones took
harsher treatment. Henry Gannon owned a few tame oxen;
some of the *ladinos,* the wildest outlaws, would be necked
to these, and after as much as a week the oxen would fight
them into submission and bring them in. Others had to be
starved until they could hardly walk, and the worst had
their eyelids sewed shut so they were blinded; Calhoon
had watched incredulously as Gannon and Elias and the
others performed this operation. One way or another,
though, the Texans always brought them in.

Still, there were some old mossyhorns that refused to
yield, the unreformable bunch-quitters and the killers.
These Gannon quickly spotted and shot, and they furnished beef for the cow crowd.

With all this every animal brought in represented hard
work and sacrifice and danger; and each one was precious.
The herd at South Springs and the other pen represented
the lives of men, laid on the line for property. So Calhoon,
keeping the brand books, was meticulous.

But as the herd grew, their problems had increased. It
took roughly one man for each hundred cattle to handle a
gather of such size, which meant riders had to be taken off
active cowhunting to watch the cattle they had already
caught. Before long they would have reached the point of
diminishing returns if it had not been for the new recruits.

A couple drifted in every day, sometimes white, sometimes blacks, not a few Mexicans. Though none of the
Rancho Bravo men had been back to town, word seemed
to float on the wind: something big was going on at Henry
Gannon's ranch. Now more than thirty Texans were scattered over Gannon's range, each working demonically to
build his own herd. And, Calhoon thought, crushing out
the cigarette against the saddle horn, there were still two
months left. At this rate, when the tax deadline fell, Weymouth might gain the land, but there would be precious
few cattle on it.

His rest over, Calhoon lifted the reins. Riding on, he
never relaxed his alertness. So far, perhaps because of
Killraine and his soldiers, maybe because Weymouth had

other plans, or because the Regulators would not work with Isaacs and their other leaders in jail, his patrolling had been in vain. There had been no trouble.

But he had fought too long and too hard not to recognize this quiet as only the lull before the storm. Unless Joshua Weymouth were vastly different from his son, sooner or later the cyclone would come; and when it did, it would be tremendous.

Chapter 7

For another week the uneasy peace endured. The herd grew, a great colorful splotch against the dun grass, its components black, white, brown, brindle, piebald, roan; and every day dozens more of the resisting cattle were driven or dragged into the pens. Calhoon patrolled ceaselessly, alertly, but found no sign of strangers on the range.

Prowling the brush was hot and weary business, and he was tired that night as he emerged from the shinnery on to the great prairie where the cattle were held. Beyond the pens campfire smoke made a gray finger against the crimson of the sunset, and the west wind brought the smell of growing things and dust and longhorns, all combined into a strange, tangy, stirring perfume that touched something deep within him as he loped toward the fire. This Rancho Bravo, he thought. It was becoming something real, magnificent. He would have to be careful, remember that it was not his dream but Henry Gannon's and Elias Whitton's, and he was only using it. He must not let it weaken him or interfere with what he had come here to do, when the time came to do it.

Always the cavalryman, when he reached the fire, he saw to his horse first, giving it a rub, checking it for thorns, turning it into the rope corral. Only then did he join Gannon, Whitton, and a few other men where beef roasted over the embers.

"Loosh," Henry said, "everything quiet?"

"Like a grave." Calhoon squatted.

Elias spat into the fire. "Seem like Weymouth playin' mighty close to his vest. You reckon there cards up his sleeve?"

"Maybe," Henry said. "Or maybe it ain't worth it to

him to raise a fuss with Gordon away and Isaacs in the calaboose. After all, the range will still fall to him when tax time come, and when you git down to it, what use are the cattle with no market for 'em here?"

"He smart enough to know there be a market someday, and he got money enough to be able to afford to hold 'em. Anyhow," Elias went on, "if all we was doin' was gatherin' mesquite beans, Josh Weymouth would still begrudge us because in a couple of months they'd be *his* mesquite beans."

Henry stared into the flame. "Well, maybe if I was in his boots, I'd feel the same. It's funny, 'Lias, Loosh, but I can remember when I was little and Josh useta hold me on his knee. After all, he had a big spread of his own, and he was our closest neighbor, and him and my old man *had* to work together on cow hunts and drives; and they fought Injuns together. Then it musta seemed to Josh that everything hit him all at once. First off, Miz Weymouth died, left him alone with Gordon to raise." He looked at Calhoon. "I reckon that's how come Gordon grew up like he did. Josh had already lost two other kids when they was little, and Gordon was all he had left. He just mortally worshipped that boy and still does. I reckon he spoiled him pretty bad. He never laid a hand on him or said nay to him about anything, and back when ever'body had a little money, he always seen to it that Gordon rode the best horse and wore the fanciest outfit and owned the finest gun that cash could buy. The result bein', naturally, that Gordon grew up mean as a snake; me, I had to whip him once or twice myself . . . Nobody could stand Gordon, and Josh knew it, and yet he couldn't bring hisself to jerk a knot in him, make a man of him." He shuttled his gaze to Calhoon's wrist. "So you paid the price of that," he said.

"I don't care how he got that way," Calhoon said coldly.

"No. I'm just trying to explain. Then on top of everything else, he and my daddy fell out over politics." Henry grinned faintly, ruefully. "You'da had to know my old man to understand what he put Weymouth through. Daddy was a hard man and Secesh and States' Rights to the core, and the minute Josh spoke out for the Union, Daddy went after him, friendship or no. He had the whole territory behind him, and Josh couldn't fight 'em all. Finally he and Gordon had to run, I mean, to save their lives. Feelings was so high against the Union that both of 'em might have swung from a live oak if they hadn't hightailed it. So I reckon Josh figures now he's just gettin' back his own—not for himself but for Gordon."

He paused. "I don't begrudge him the land, in a way. It's almost like he's due it, and besides, I wouldn't keep it even if I could. Not with those high plains waitin' out yonder. But I'll fight him for the cattle. I—" He broke off, looking toward the west. "Rider comin'."

"All ours in, I think," Elias Whitton said and got to his feet. Calhoon also arose, turning toward the distant drum of hoofbeats, one horseman, coming fast.

Then the mounted man swept from behind a thicket and galloped across the open, stocky and clad in blue; and they all recognized that compact figure. "Killraine," Elias said. "And like his shirttail on fire. This ain't his day to inspect the guard, neither."

They looked at one another, and Calhoon saw the same apprehension written on his partner's faces that he felt himself. None of them moved until Killraine, slowing his mount, trotted up to the fire. "Gentlemen," he said, reining in.

"Light and rest, Captain," Henry said cordially.

Killraine swung down, stripping off his gauntlets. His swarthy face was grave, his eyes troubled as he looked about him. "Gannon, Whitton, Calhoon. I'd like to talk to the three of you privately."

"Sho," Henry said easily. "Over yonder under that big mesquite." He motioned to the lacy shade of an ancient tree, and when they were beneath it, Henry asked, "Well, Captain, what's on your mind?"

"Several things, none of them good." Killraine took out a cigar, bit off its end, clamped it between his teeth, and lighted it, all the while appraising the herd and the pens. Then, briskly he said, "Isaacs is on the loose."

"What?" Calhoon frowned.

"I told you I'd hold him and his men for instructions from General Sheridan. Today I got word: release them without further investigation or prosecution." He shrugged. "Pressure from Washington, of course. Gordon's there now and practically in bed with Grant. Anyhow, I turned Isaacs and the others loose a while ago."

"Thanks for telling us," Calhoon said. "We'll keep a sharp lookout."

Killraine rolled the cigar across his mouth. "That's not all of it. There's more to come." His eyes raked across them. "You know that Josh Weymouth's also chairman of the county board of supervisors."

"So?" Gannon asked tensely.

"So they met this morning. And passed an ordinance." Killraine took the cigar from his mouth. "Gannon, how many men have you got working for you who hold brands in their own names?"

"Thirty-one," Henry said.

Killraine looked down at his boots. "Three hundred ten dollars," he muttered.

"What?" Henry's voice rose. "Cap'n, what the hell you talkin' about?"

"The county supervisors," Killraine said, raising his head. "They're all Weymouth's men anyhow. So they held a meeting this morning and passed an ordinance. From now on, to register a brand costs ten dollars in this county. And . . . the ordinance is retroactive for thirty days." His green eyes swept across them. "Thirty-one brands, three hundred ten dollars. That's what they've got to pay the county, or none of the cattle they've branded belong to them."

In the twilight the wild cattle in the pens bawled hideously. A soft breeze ruffled the feathery mesquite limbs overhead. Otherwise, for a half minute there was no sound. Then Henry said, voice strangled, "Three hundred and— Cripes, there ain't that many pennies among us, let alone dollars."

"I'm sorry," Killraine said. "It gives every brand owner

who's filed a brand within the past month a week to pay. Otherwise, the brand is null and void. Anybody can file it, pay the fee, and claim every head of cattle wearing it. Your Rancho Bravo brand's safe, of course. It was filed long before the extent of the ordinance. But the brands of all these other men— If there are thirty-one, you've got to come up with over three hundred and ten dollars or—"

"Or," Calhoon said, "Weymouth's men take title to them and all the cattle wearing them."

"That's not impossible." Killraine looked at his boots again.

Gannon shifted weight. "All those men own is their cattle," he said angrily. "Cow brutes they've fought like hell to drag outa the brush. Now each one got to pay ten dollars, or his stock is gone?"

"That's the size of it, I'm afraid," Killraine said, still not meeting their eyes. "Of course, you've got a week to raise the money in."

Calhoon spat an obscenity. "As well expect us to raise the dead."

Elias Whitton's eyes glittered. "There goan be some dead, all right, soon as our men git this word. Come daybreak, they be in Double Oaks and burn that courthouse down and maybe Weymouth in it!"

Killraine whirled on him. "Is that a threat, Mr. Whitton? I assure you, if they try it, they'll run head-on into the United States Army."

"Then too damned bad for the US Army!" Henry Gannon flared. "These men have fought your Yankee army before, Killraine!" He chopped the air with his hand. "They've worked like slaves, fought the brush, risked their lives against the cattle on my say-so, that they'd be paid in stock of their own. Now you tell me no, unless they got ten dollars each. Well, Killraine, I'll tell you this. You better go back and inform your feller Union man, ole Josh Weymouth, that he'd better unpass that ordinance and damn quick, or tomorrow there won't be enough left of him to draw a buzzard!"

"If you mean a mass assault on Double Oaks, sir,"

Killraine snapped, "you'll have my men to contend with. You'll either die or wind up fugitives from justice!"

"Hell," Gannon roared, "what are we now? Where's the damned justice?" He leaned forward, face savage. "We've fought your blasted bluebellies plenty of times and made 'em howl for mercy!"

Calhoon seized his shoulder. "Henry, quit it!" He jerked Gannon back.

Henry whirled on him. "What—?"

"It's not Killraine's fault, don't you see? He's done all he can—'

"That don't change things," Gannon snapped. "When these Texans find out, it don't change nothing!" He turned on Killraine. "They'll still be comin' down on you, and I couldn't stop 'em even I wanted to!" Suddenly he whirled and, in his fury, slammed his fist against the mesquite trunk. "Goddamnit!" he said thickly.

Killraine stood there tight lipped. His eyes ranged from one to the other; only Calhoon met them directly. Then the captain let out a long, sighing breath. "Very well," he said. "Then it's up to me, I guess."

Calhoon asked quietly, "What is up to you?"

Killraine looked at him, pleading for understanding. "Somebody's got to stop it," he said thinly. Then his own self-control gave way. "Goddamnit, you think I like this, forced into pulling Weymouth's rotten chestnuts out of the fire?" He slapped his gauntlets furiously into the other hand. "Compared to this, the war was clean and simple. At least, by God, you knew who was on your side and who wasn't!" Then he broke off, and his next words were calmer. "All right, Calhoon. I suppose it's the only way. I'll lend your Rancho Bravo the money."

"You'll what?" Lucius Calhoon stared.

"Damnit, I said I'll lend you the money! Three hundred and ten—hell, make it three fifty to round it out. It's better than having to fight those damned wild Texans of yours in the streets of Double Oaks. Your people are seasoned veterans, most of my command's green as grass.

And I'll be damned if I'll see them killed to line Weymouth's pockets. So I'll make you the loan!"

"Hell, we can't—" Henry shook his head violently.

"Hush." Lucius Calhoon fixed Killraine with his eyes. "Captain, do you mean this?"

"Do you know of any other way of stopping a bloodbath?" Killraine said wearily. "A head-on collision between your men and mine? With nobody winning but Joshua Weymouth?"

"No," Calhoon said, "I don't. I've worked with these men long enough to know them now, and what Henry says is true. Very well . . . Your offer's accepted. Have you got the money with you?"

"Of course not. I'll have to cash a bank draft tomorrow, but I'll have it by ten o'clock."

"I'll be there then at your office in town."

"Only," Killraine said, "if you come alone. One soldier for escort; no more. I'll not have that whole bunch of Texas hellions pouring into town, spoiling for a fight. I'll guarantee your safety there and back here again. But the deal is off if you cause any violence. Now, I'll bid you good day." Brusquely he turned away.

Gannon watched him stride toward his horse. "Killraine!"

The officer turned.

"I—" Henry made an ineffectual gesture.

Killraine laughed without humor. "Don't get carried away with gratitude. Remember, I'm a Yankee and a New Englander at that. One of those who, I believe your Texas folklore has it, sells wooden nutmegs and cares for nothing but the almighty dollar. Never fear, Gannon, I'll get my money's worth somehow." Then he mounted, wheeled the horse, and galloped off.

As he rode across the prairie, circling wide of the herd, Henry Gannon said wonderingly, "He's some little rooster, ain't he? I wonder what's his game."

"He a lot of man," Elias murmured. "That his game." He walked back to the fire and the others followed him. "So Isaacs on the loose again. And it turn out I right:

Weymouth, he got plenty high cards up his sleeve. Looks like he really draw some water up in Washington, or Gordon does. Henry, we got to double our guard on that herd tonight."

"Elias is right," Calhoon said. "All the same, I've got a feeling that Isaacs won't hit us right away. Weymouth will be waiting to see what happens when we find out about those brand fees. Likely he's hoping that just what Killraine was afraid of will happen. Our men find out about 'em, not have a chance of payin' 'em, and blow up and hit town on the prod, ready to burn the place down. Then Killraine would have to fight us, and we'd chew each other up while Weymouth stands clear and laughs."

"Well, that won't happen now, thanks to that little Yankee," Gannon said.

"But Weymouth doesn't know that yet. He'll find out tomorrow, though, and that's when we've got to worry."

"All the same," Elias said, "we're takin' no chances with that herd. And you, Calhoon—since you got to be in town tomorrow, I'll scout the brush tonight myself." He grinned. "Them Regulators—Kansas and Missouri men. They don't know beans about the shinnery. If Isaacs send any of 'em out there to watch us, by tomorrow mornin' I may have some scalps."

"Scalps?" Calhoon blurted.

Elias, still grinning, drew his knife and ran his thumb along the edge. "They come in handy when we back among the Comanch'. Them folks respect a man with a big string of somebody else's hair." Then he sheathed the blade, went toward his horse. "I make a little circle now." While Henry Gannon and Lucius Calhoon stared at one another, he mounted and rode away.

The next morning at ten, with the corporal by his side Calhoon rode into Double Oaks; and when he passed The Texas Flag, Isaacs was on the porch.

He still bore the marks of the fight: a nose even more purplish and permanently smeared sideways, so that now he was remarkably ugly. As he saw the riders coming, he walked to the edge of the porch and stood there with both hands close to his guns. But he said nothing, made no farther move. His eyes met Calhoon's, and his lips drew back from his teeth; and Calhoon said quietly to the corporal, "Watch my back." He was glad he had the soldier with him; the blue uniform was like a shield.

But Isaacs was, for now, apparently on a leash. Likely Calhoon thought, he would not be that way for long. Presently The Texas Flag was lost to sight behind the plaza's cottonwoods, and Calhoon sheathed the rifle he had carried across his saddle. At the courthouse hitchrack he pulled up and swung down. "Watch my horse," he said, "and don't let anybody tamper with that gun."

Entering the corridor, he caught sight of Joshua Weymouth through an open door. The tall, gray-maned man was talking to a clerk; but he saw Calhoon passing and straightened up. Calhoon was aware of Weymouth's stepping out into the corridor and watching him as he entered Killraine's office.

Inside the door he halted. Killraine's suite was two rooms, and Evelyn emerged from the inner one, a sheaf of papers in her hands. Morning sun struck reddish gleams from her luxurious hair; the dress of dotted Swiss she wore was modest, yet somehow emphasized the rounded beauty of her upper body. Something inside Calhoon seemed to leap, and he felt an inexplicable tightening in his throat.

She smiled. "Good morning, Captain Calhoon. Philip said he was expecting you. He's in his office." She gestured with the papers. "I've been helping him with some personal correspondence."

"Thank you, Miss Killraine." Calhoon took off his hat. He started for the other door, and her voice stopped him. "Oh, Captain."

"Yes?" He turned.

"Perhaps after you've finished your business with Phil, you'll join us for lunch? Our house is just down the street. I imagine you're tired of beef, and I have a lovely hen to bake."

"Miss Killraine, that's the best news I've heard in years. I'd be delighted."

"About noon then, Captain. Phil will bring you."

"Yes, ma'am." Then he entered Killraine's office.

Killraine was behind the desk, and he looked up, leaned back. "Well, Calhoon, I see you made it."

"I might not have without the corporal. Isaacs and most of his crew were at The Texas Flag."

"He didn't actually threaten you?"

"No."

"Good. I warned him before I turned him loose not to cause any trouble, for whatever effect it might have. Sit down, Calhoon." He motioned to a chair and, as the South Carolinian took it, opened a drawer, brought out a canvas bag that clinked when he dropped it on the desk. "There you are. Three hundred fifty dollars in gold. Better count it."

Calhoon opened the bag, spread out the coins, then nodded, putting them in his pocket. "And the note?"

"Here." Killraine passed over a piece of paper.

Calhoon read it. "You've got no particular date for repayment."

The captain grinned. "Do you know when you'll have three hundred and fifty dollars, cash?"

"No," Calhoon said.

Killraine shrugged. "So— When and if you get the money—" He met Calhoon's eyes. "I'm not worried Calhoon. If I haven't learned to judge men by now—"

Calhoon reached for the pen, signed the note, passed it back. "Killraine, what can I say—?"

"Nothing." Killraine leaned back, face stern. "I fought you people, you Southerners, for four damned long years; and we won and you lost, and to a soldier that's the end of it. I just want to see this country reunited now, and I intend to use what little power I have in what little area I command, plus what little personal wealth I own, to make things work like that." He turned in the chair, stared out the window.

"So damned many good men dead," he said softly, "and it's like spitting on their graves when a man like Weymouth uses their deaths to get fat . . ." Then he came alert again and bounced out of his chair. "Very well, Calhoon;

suppose we go now and register our brands. I'll accompany you personally."

"Right." Calhoon followed him out of the office and down the hall. He noticed that Evelyn had left.

Killraine led him to another office with a sign: Deed, Land and Brand Registration. There was a counter piled with ledgers and a rabbity-faced, middle-aged clerk wearing a green eye shade behind it. "Good morning, Captain," he said cordially enough. "And you, sir." His voice was less cordial at the sight of the Confederate hat.

From his pocket Calhoon took a small notebook of the kind Gannon used for keeping tally. Opening it, he laid it on the counter. "I understand you folks are charging ten bucks each for brands registered during the last month. I want to pay the fees for these thirty-one brands—and I want a separate receipt for each one."

"Why—" The clerk bent over the notebook. His nose began to twitch as he read. Then he straightened up. "Just a minute. I mean—" He reached for the notebook, but Calhoon clamped a hand over it. "I'll have to go see—" the clerk said, and he scurried out through a side door.

Calhoon and Killraine looked at one another, and the captain smiled beneath his waxed moustache. "This is why I came with you. I figured you might have a little, ah, administrative trouble."

Then the clerk was back, his face pale. "I'm sorry," he said in a quivering voice, "but the office is closing for dinner. You'll have to come back later on."

Calhoon hauled out his watch. "Eleven o'clock. You people eat early."

"It's . . . it's . . ." The man's voice trailed off as he looked into Calhoon's eyes. "I can't help it," he finished. "We're closing, that's all. Come back at, say, two o'clock."

"No," Calhoon said. "Because something might happen. Like, for instance, somebody else registering these same brands and paying the money while I was gone. And that—" he leaned closer to the clerk "—would make me mighty, mighty unhappy with you, you understand?"

"I—" The man licked his lips. Then suddenly he raised

his head, and his face registered relief. "Judge Weymouth," he said gratefully.

Calhoon and Captain Killraine turned around. Weymouth stood there in the office door, his eyes like beads of jet, shuttling from one to the other. "What's the matter, Greene, you having problems?" he asked in that deep voice. "Gentlemen, didn't you hear Mr. Greene? He's closing his office until two."

Killraine said, "The hours of this office are from eight until noon and from one until five."

"Captain," Weymouth said, "do you have a brand to register?"

"No."

"Then I'd advise you to stay out of this. And you, Mr. . . . Calhoon, isn't it?"

"That's right."

"If you'll be back at two, we'll accommodate you as best we can. You understand that all fees are payable in US currency or gold?"

"I'm prepared to pay them in gold," Calhoon said. He reached in his pockets, brought out a handful of double eagles.

Weymouth looked surprised; then he frowned, turning his glance thoughtfully to Killraine. "Ahh," he said gustily. "You—"

"Texas," Killraine said easily, "is the coming state. Or so I always hear. Thought I'd do well to make a small investment in it."

"You would do well, Captain Killraine, to attend to your duties and stay out of matters that don't concern you."

"This matter concerns me deeply, Judge. You could say, in fact, it means the difference between peace and war here on the streets of Double Oaks. The difference—" Killraine's voice grated "—between life and death for some of my troopers." And now he flung the command angrily. "I want those fees paid and receipted for immediately, before this office closes for any reason whatsoever, and I assure you, sir, that if that does not happen, I'll take it on myself to impound the books of this office until two o'clock with whatever force is necessary!"

"You wouldn't dare!" Weymouth snapped.

"You'd be surprised what I'd dare." Killraine's voice was low and scathing now. "Judge, I'm no babe in the woods. I've pulled a lot of duty in a lot of different places in my time, and I've seen a lot of politics and a deal of corruption. But I'll confess, sir, duty here in Double Oaks has been a revelation. So if I have to adapt my tactics to yours to carry out my orders, I will. Either this man's business is taken care of right now, or I'll have an armed detail take these books at once."

Their eyes locked, and then to the surprise of Calhoon and the captain both, Joshua Weymouth smiled. "Why, Captain," he said, "don't get so worked up. In the long run it doesn't make any difference, does it? If that's the way you want it— Greene, accept Mr. Calhoon's payments and give him a separate receipt for each. Make sure he's completely satisfied before he leaves, you hear?"

The clerk goggled. "Yes, sir."

"Of course, Killraine," Weymouth continued easily, "you're not to think you scared me. It so happens that your impounding the books would have been a loose end I don't want dangling, so . . . You'll be in town this afternoon, Captain Killraine? Where you can be reached?"

Killraine frowned. "I'll be here."

"Good," Weymouth said. "I think we'll be conferring later on today. If things work out, you may even have a little surprise in store for you." He turned to the clerk. "Go ahead, Greene, get to work." He turned, strode out.

To his back Killraine said, "Weymouth! Wait a minute!"

"Just be patient, Captain," Weymouth said, not turning. "Be patient and all your troubles with me will be at an end." Then he was gone.

"More pie, Captain Calhoon? There's plenty left and what about some coffee?"

The house Philip Killraine shared with his sister was

small, its rented furniture undistinguished, but Evelyn Killraine had put a distinct mark upon it with curtains and flowers, making it both restful and attractive. Lucius Calhoon leaned back in his chair at the dining table and shook his head. "I couldn't manage another bite. And believe me, I regret it, because you're a fine cook. I didn't know Northern women had it in them." And he grinned.

"I'm not much with sowbelly and black-eyed peas, true. But I do have my little specialties." Her smile had a way of lighting her eyes. "Tell me, Captain Calhoon, what's a cow hunt like?"

"Pretty rough. Come out sometime to Gannon's ranch and I'll show you. You can't go out in the brush, but you can see the herd, and a thousand or so cattle in one bunch is quite a sight."

"I'll bet it is. Phil, will you take me sometime this week?"

"It depends," Killraine said absently.

"Phil, what's into you anyhow?" She frowned. "You've been miles away all through the meal."

"Nothing," Killraine said a little irritably. But it was true; he had been moody and silent since they had left the courthouse. That vague statement of Weymouth was bothering him profoundly, Calhoon saw, and he himself felt a certain apprehension. Then he turned back to the girl.

"Anyhow, Miss Killraine—"

"Don't you think we could make it Evelyn? And—Lucius, isn't it?"

"That suits me fine. Anyhow, when you get a chance, come out, I'll show you around. I'll guarantee this; it won't be like Connecticut."

"Oh . . . Connecticut. You know, it seems so little and prissy now after having been in Texas. Phil and I've been talking. We hope he's stationed here a long time."

"So do I," Calhoon said.

Killraine shoved back his chair. "Calhoon, I hate to rush you, but I think it would be a good idea if you and Corporal Sondergaard got back to Rancho Bravo well before dark."

"Phil—" the girl said.

But Killraine looked significantly at Calhoon's shirt pocket. In it were thirty-one receipts for the registration of brands. "You wouldn't want to lose what you came here for."

"No, I wouldn't. You think Weymouth might—?"

"I don't know what Weymouth will do. All I know is that he's up to something, and if I were you, I'd ride."

"Yes. Well, Evelyn, I'll say again—" Calhoon pushed back his chair, was just standing up when somebody hammered on the front door.

Nervously Killraine spun around. "Who's that?" He strode across the living room, opened the door.

The voice of Joshua Weymouth came from the doorway. "Captain, may I come in?"

"Of course," Killraine said and stepped aside, and Weymouth entered. Calhoon stared at the man with him. He was short, silver haired, and potbellied, with a doughy face. And his uniform was that of a captain of United States Cavalry.

"Captain Philip Killraine," Weymouth said, satisfaction written large all over his wolfish face, "meet Captain Daniel Potter. He just came in on the one o'clock stage from Galveston with orders from Colonel Granger there to relieve you of command immediately and take over your troop himself."

Chapter 8

Two hours later Calhoon, riding secret ways through the brush, skulking like a wolf, had no escort, no trooper to accompany him. Captain Daniel Potter had seen to that immediately.

There had been a moment of stunned silence in the living room. Then Evelyn Killraine's voice had broken it. "Oh, no!"

"Hush, Ev," her brother said. "Potter. You have written orders?" Almost absently he took the captain's puffy hand and shook it.

"Of course." Potter drew papers from his blouse. "Here you are, Killraine. You'll be transferred to duty on the Kansas frontier. You're to relinquish command to me upon receipt of these orders and prepare to depart immediately."

Killraine, reading the papers, said nothing. Then he folded them. "Very well." His voice was bitter. He looked at Weymouth. "This was your important business?"

"I wasn't sure whether the stage would be on time or not," Weymouth said. "As it turned out, it was." He smiled, eyes glittering with triumph. "I should have closed the brand office and let you impound the books, Captain. You would only have held them for an hour . . . Well, no matter. We'll miss you, of course . . ." His voice was thick with sarcasm.

"I believe, Captain, that we can transact all business very quickly," Potter said. "I want all men on detached duty, wherever they may be, brought in for roll call and inspection, and I'll go over your accounts and records this afternoon. By tomorrow you should be free to depart for your next station, assuming everything's in order—and I'm sure it will be."

"Oh, it will be," Weymouth said. "Captain Killraine's very meticulous."

"Can you meet me at your office in a half-hour, Captain?" Potter asked.

"I'll be there," Killraine said.

"Very well. Judge Weymouth has already obtained quarters for me—very nice ones, I might add . . ." He smiled at Weymouth. "So there'll be no trouble there. Sorry to have interrupted your meal, but as your men will find out, I like things done promptly and done right."

"Yeah," Killraine said. "Yeah, I'll bet you do."

Potter looked at him a moment, then said to Weymouth, "Well, Judge, shall we go?"

Weymouth looked over Killraine's head at Lucius Calhoon. "Yes," he said. "Come along." And the two of them went out, closing the door behind them.

"Oh, Phil," Evelyn Killraine said sickly.

Killraine snorted so hard his moustache fluttered. "There you are. Gordon Weymouth's fine Italian hand in Washington. No wonder his father looked like the cat that had swallowed the canary this morning. Loosh—" He spread his hands. "Corporal Sondergaard will have to stay here, and I'll have to ask you to send in the other two troopers from Gannon's ranch. Whitton will have to reapply to Captain Potter for protection. But if I were you, I wouldn't count on his getting it."

"No," Calhoon said. "This rips it, doesn't it? Gives Weymouth a free hand."

"He'll turn Isaacs and the Regulators loose like so many wolves," Killraine said. "And Potter will probably look the other way. If Weymouth weren't sure of that, he wouldn't have been assigned here."

"Phil, isn't there *something* you can do?" Evelyn asked, wringing her hands.

"He's done all and more for us than we could have expected," Calhoon said. "Don't ruin your career or mess up your record on our account, Phil."

"I'll worry about my career. What you'd better worry

about, Loosh, are those receipts you've got in your pocket. You'll be traveling back to your herd alone and— I've got a hunch Weymouth has no idea of letting you deliver them to your men."

"The same hunch occurred to me," Calhoon said. "I'm going to ask you one more favor. Will you ride with me out of town as far as the edge of the shinnery? Once I get into the brush, I'm all right, but it would be mighty easy for Isaacs and his men to pick a gunfight with me before I get there, and I wouldn't stand much chance alone in the open against 'em."

"I'll ride with you," Killraine said. He went to a hat tree, took his belt from it, buckled on his Colt, clapped on his hat. "As far as you want me to go. Let Potter wait."

"Only to the brush. But we'd better strike out now. Evelyn, I'm sorry—"

"So am I." She came to him, took his left hand. "Kansas," she said bitterly. Then she was looking up at Calhoon with green eyes, and her voice was throaty and taut. "Lucius, be careful, do you understand? Very careful. We . . . we'll try to see you before we go."

Go. For the first time Calhoon really understood that she would be leaving, that this was part of it all. That thought was like a blow low in the belly. "I'll be careful," he said. "And yes. One way or the other I'll see you before you go."

She held his hand a moment longer, then released it. "Good luck," she said and turned away.

Calhoon stood fixed for a few seconds more. Then Killraine's voice sliced into his consciousness. "All right, Loosh. Let's get your horse and ride . . ."

At the brush he and Killraine had shaken hands. "Like Evelyn said," the captain told him, "we'll see you before we leave."

"Good. I'll need an address to send the money to."

"The hell with the money," Killraine said bitterly. "Watch your flanks." Then he wheeled and galloped off.

Wasting no time watching him go, Calhoon had put the Morgan in the brush after a glance at the sun to orient

himself. Despite all Killraine's efforts, it was war now, indeed; and Weymouth would open it by doing his best to
keep those receipts out of their owners' hands. The only
way to do that was to intercept Lucius Calhoon, blow him
out of the saddle, and take them from him.

But first, Calhoon thought, they were going to have to
find him. The chaparral was no longer strange to him;
after weeks of scouting it, he knew something of its ways
and how to work through it off the trails. It would take a
long time and be rough on man and horse alike, but it was
safer than following the high roads and main paths that
would take him to the herd by the shortest route. All the
same, he had to make it before dark. With the soldiers
gone, Isaacs had a free hand to strike, and Calhoon doubt-
ed he would waste much time doing it. As Elias had said,
it would be no trick to stampede the herd from hell to
breakfast and bring all the work of nearly a month to
nothing.

So urgency rode with him, even as he slithered through
the thickets like a wild bull himself, keeping always to
cover, traveling as silently as possible. He made a wide
swing, presently came to the edge of the eastbound road,
scouted it from the brush's edge before he crossed it at a
run, and vanished once more in the shinnery. Again, guid-
ing by dead reckoning, using whatever remote cattle trails
he found, he worked his way through great thickets of
mesquite, black chaparral, catclaw, and prickly pear.
Sometimes he could see the sun; at other times the whole
sky was blanked out by the canopy of brush overhead. He
circled the openings, stayed out of them, and all this took
a long time and a terrible toll of horse and rider. But there
were still a couple of hours until sundown as he neared the
main trail that led from Gannon's ranch to the South
Springs pens where the herd was held. It was tempting to
strike out of this spiked torture chamber and take the trail,
but he had no intention of doing that. A man riding it
would be absolutely defenseless against a bullet from the
brush. Instead, he paralleled it; and he had traveled not
more than a half mile that way when he saw the hawk.

Low overhead and not five hundred yards away, it

struck a small bird in an explosion of feathers. Then, prey gripped in its talons, it circled down into the bush to eat. Calhoon, reined in, letting the Morgan blow, saw it vanish behind a clump of mesquite; then, suddenly it was rising again, flapping frantically, and he heard its thin mewing cry. Calhoon frowned. To anybody who knew the outdoors, the bird's message was clear: there was something down there where it had been about to light that had frightened it. Not a longhorn or a pack of peccaries; not even a lobo wolf; perhaps a bobcat or a panther in a tree, but those animals were rare. Whatever it was in the mesquite up there, Calhoon knew he had to investigate it before riding on.

Swinging down off the Morgan, he checked the Henry and then looked very carefully to the load and caps of the Starr revolver. Although he did not like its extra weight or awkward balance compared to the Navy Colt he'd lost in the fight with Isaacs, it would have to do. He tied the Morgan to a limb large enough to hold it unless it was desperate and small enough to be broken if he did not come back. Mopping sweat from his eyes, he went ahead on foot, the Henry in his left hand.

It was at times like this that he missed the right hand badly. When catclaw and other spiked growth caught and held him, it was hard to free himself, especially without making noise. And he knew he had to proceed absolutely soundlessly.

He could not remember when he had begun to learn how to move through heavy brush in utter silence. As soon as he'd been old enough to carry a gun, his father had taken him into the Wateree and Santee canebrakes after deer and bear. He and the black man who was the plantation's chief hunter and more like an Indian in the woods than anyone Calhoon had ever known. Both men were long since dead; but both of them had drummed the secret of silent traveling into him: go slow, have patience. Take it one step at a time . . . He remembered that now, edging through the thicket; and although he might be wasting time, he would rather waste a half hour than his life.

So, carefully and inch by inch, he made his way through the brush on a beeline toward the spot where the hawk had refused to light. Ten minutes, twenty; then Calhoon crouched and held his breath.

No, he had not wasted anything. Up ahead he heard the soft plopping of a horse voiding its bowels and then its snort of relief. He froze, testing the wind. It was in his face. Sure of that, he edged on.

Then he saw the horses—two of them, tethered to a mesquite. Sorrel and bay: he made out their shaggy sides through a network of branches. Beyond them the density of the thicket lessened; the trail passed by not far away.

Calhoon considered, then moved on, swinging out wide, taking advantage of the wind so the animals could not scent him. He dodged an impenetrable clump of nopal and then he sank to his belly, the rifle cradled in his arms, and began to crawl, head and butt both low.

He took punishment, even the leather insufficient to ward off the thorns; all he could do was guard his eyes. But presently he had made his circuit; he was ahead of the horses and could see what was in front of them. There was a tiny clearing in the edge of the brush immediately at the flank of the trail, with only a screen of mesquite to shield it. The two men lay flat, close together, between the mesquite trunks, heels pointed toward him, heads away from him, watching the trail, rifles ready in their hands. The distance was not more than fifty feet. The field of fire was terrible, but there was nothing that could be done about that. In order to have a clear shot, he would simply have to stand erect.

As he did so, gingerly lining the Henry, he heard one of the bushwhackers grunt an oath. "Damn bugs eatin' us alive," he muttered. "And still the son' bitch ain't come. I think he's give us the slip."

Now Calhoon was on his feet, rifle aimed. "No, he ain't," he said in a cold voice that carried. "He's right behind you. Drop those guns and come up with hands high!"

There was one frozen second when they lay motionless. "Up!" Calhoon snapped again.

Then they were coming up all right, but with their guns.

"Get the one-handed bastard!" one yelled, and the thicket seemed to explode as he twisted, saw Calhoon, lined his gun, and fired, still on his knees. From that position his slug, too hasty, went wild, but Calhoon's well-aimed ball caught him in the chest and slammed him over backward. "Jesus!" the man screamed, and then the other Henry thundered as the second man took better aim. But Calhoon was already falling sideways, and he heard the slap of lead just by his head as he came down on one knee, throwing the Henry away, hand flashing to the Starr revolver. In a blurred motion it was up and out, and he punched off a shot at a figure jumping behind the thick trunk of a gnarled old mesquite. It was sheer luck; the .44 ball caught the man's upper arm just before it disappeared behind the tree, and the impact whirled him, threw him out from behind his cover. He screamed in agony and, one handed, tried to raise the rifle. Calhoon pulled the trigger and shot him in the belly. The heavy ball picked him up and threw him on his back. He kept on screaming, feet hammering on the ground. Calhoon fired again, aiming, and the screaming chopped off short. Then, except for the whinnying of frightened horses, everything was silent, neither figure in the grove moving or making a sound. Powder smoke floated in white clouds through the shinnery, its pungency drowning out the perfume of growing things. Calhoon, on his knees, held the pistol ready, himself shaking slightly with reaction, wondering if there were more across the trail.

Five minutes passed. The smoke drifted off; the horses quieted, save for nervous stamping. Neither body in the grove so much as twitched. At last, a little unsteadily Calhoon got to his feet but not before he had recharged the Starr and crimped new caps on its nipples.

Holstering the pistol, picking up his rifle from where he'd thrown it, he edged warily into the grove. With all the dead men he had seen, a corpse was still no sight to take any satisfaction in, and he grimaced as he went from one to the other. His first shot had killed almost instantly; the second man, who'd taken three rounds, was a sodden mess, face contorted in death agony.

Quickly Calhoon went to work. He salvaged gunbelts, pistols and shot pouches; one of the ambushers carried a Navy Colt exactly like the one he'd lost, and he substituted that and its holster for the Starr, preferring its lighter weight and better balance. It was necessary to go through their pockets, too; he did not disturb whatever papers they had, but Rancho Bravo was entitled to and could use the forty dollars he took off one and the twenty the other body yielded, as well as their rifles and cartridges and the two horses and their gear; horses were vital, and they were short of them.

When he'd picked them clean, he shook out a riata taken from one of their saddles, looped one body's leg and then the other. Mounted, he dragged the corpses deep into the brush at rope's end, and when he shook off the rope, they were hidden by a tangle of black chaparral, as invisible and lost as if buried at sea. He went back to the Morgan, leading the extra horse, gathered the Morgan up to lead as well, and edged through the brush to the trail. Then, gambling that these two had been all there were, he rode hard toward the South Springs Pen. Down the trail he halted once, looked back. Already in the evening sky black specks circled. Two days, three, and the vultures, wolves, and coyotes, even the javelinas, would clean the bones . . .

Henry Gannon's eyes were sunken deep in his head; his whole body was lax with weariness, as he stood by the campfire, listening to Lucius Calhoon. For weeks now, months, he had been working at a pace almost superhuman, and it had taken its toll. There was a curious lack of spirit in him as he sighed and spat into the embers.

"Well, you done good, Loosh. You done pulled about as much fat out of the fire as one man could. Only—' He looked across the twilit prairie to the great herd. "Only, damnit, we're in for it now. I didn't know how much I've been counting on Killraine all along. Now he's gone, and Weymouth's free to cut loose his wolf and not have to answer to anybody." He jerked his head. "He can scatter this herd from hell to breakfast, spooky as it is, and no way we can stop him. Then all that work shot to nothing."

"Not all of it," Elias said. "At least them cattle branded now. And herdbroke enough so we don't have to fight ever' one of 'em to bring 'em in if they run."

"But he can keep on doin' it over and over. Make 'em wild again and meanwhile, we're pinned down trying to watch 'em. A couple of rifle shots, somebody bangin' on a tin pan, anything at all, especially at night, and they're off and gone. The son of a bitch has got us over a barrel."

"Maybe," Lucius Calhoon said. "And maybe not." He tossed a cigarette butt into the fire. "Henry, you're beat down, and you're not thinkin' straight. Has it occurred to you that if we play our cards right, when Isaacs comes this could be our chance to finish him once and for all and get him off our necks?"

Gannon stared at him. "Loosh, what you mean? I don't think you understand the situation."

"I understand this," Calhoon said. "The only way you can beat your enemy is to fight him. Bring him to battle. And on *your* battleground, not his."

Whitton's eyes gleamed. "Go on, Loosh."

"Henry's thinking just like Weymouth wants him to think. Me, I say the quicker Isaacs comes, the better. We want him to come soon, and we want him to come hard with *all* his Regulators. Then—and only then—can we chop him down. Hell, now we've got as many men as he has."

"That means nothing," Henry snapped. "Our men have to guard the herd. And once it's runnin'— You never been in a stampede. Believe me, when a big herd goes, there ain't no time for fightin', unless you want to lose it."

"Then we'll lose it," Calhoon said harshly.

"Loosh—" Gannon sprang to his feet.

"Wait a minute, Henry." Whitton also arose. "Me, I think I hear a horse soldier talkin', and he's got something up his sleeve. Calhoon, you go on."

"It's a long chance," Lucius Calhoon began. "But if it works, it'll wipe out the Regulators, and before Weymouth can hire more of their stripe, Rancho Bravo'll be on the trail. Listen—" and they bent close to him as he went on talking.

Chapter 9

The enormous pall of smoke was a gigantic smudge against the dying light of day's end, huge enough to be visible for miles. Looking at it, Calhoon felt a certain sadness. Animals would die in that great brush fire: the slow-footed, slow-witted ones anyhow, like armadillos and possums; most, though, would escape, dashing from the thickets along with the dozens of longhorns holed up in there. But there was no help for it; that great pyre was necessary.

Although it was far from the flats below, the cattle down there were restless. Calhoon saw how hard the men had to work to hold the herd, and the ones in the pens of mesquite poles, the wilder ones, recently driven in there to starve until tame, raised a hideous bawling. Calhoon only hoped the pens would hold.

He lifted rein, put the Morgan into motion, jogging along a trail through the brush rimming the prairie on which the herd was held. When he reached high ground, he reined in, and he called softly, " 'Lias?"

The answer came from a clump of mesquite. "We here, Loosh."

Calhoon rode on into the mesquite grove. There Whitton with a half dozen men behind him waited patiently while saddled and bitted horses, tied up short, stamped and switched flies.

Calhoon surveyed the men. Every one of them, like himself, was without a hat.

"All in order?" he asked Elias.

Whitton grinned and stroked his rifle. "Let 'em come. The moon be full tonight."

"I hope they do come," Calhoon said. "But if not tonight, maybe tomorrow."

"We kin wait," Elias said. He looked toward the great cloud of smoke on the horizon. "That some fire." His black face split in a grin. "Jest like old times. You know what, Loosh? I think if this turns out all right, you done hit on a way that'll make gatherin' cattle a whole lot easier."

"Except for your stories, I'd never have thought of it."

"Yeah," Elias said. "Same way the Comanch' used to burn the prairie to drive the buffalo where they wanted 'em. Well, longhorns as wild as any buffs, and same thing holds true. Burn their cover, then you can handle 'em in the open. Anyhow, we all set here. You go check them men across the way."

"Yeah," Calhoon said. "And remember. In the dark, when the shooting starts, watch for the hats." He rode on.

A quarter of a mile away, also on high ground west of the herd, the next half dozen men, hatless, under the leadership of a lanky Texan named Webb Peters, waited just as patiently. "When you think they'll come?" Peters asked, lantern jaw moving regularly with his cud of tobacco.

"Anytime after dark," Calhoon said. And then he made sure once more that Peters knew exactly what he was to do. Convinced the Texan understood thoroughly, he swung out of the brush, put the Morgan down the hill toward the herd.

Henry Gannon saw him coming and loped his mount out to meet him. "Loosh. Tonight. You really think it'll be tonight?"

Calhoon shrugged. "It's got to be soon. All we can do is wait, hope, and keep our powder dry."

Gannon looked toward the smoke. "All the same, burning good range . . ."

"It'll grow back. And anyhow, it's not your range."

"I keep forgettin' that. When you're born and raised on a place, I reckon it's impossible not to think of it as yours for the rest of your life. But what the hell—"

"Listen," Calhoon said. "You're sure you and your men all understand now. When they hit, you're not to worry about the herd. You let it run, and you move in and fight."

"Don't worry. We'll carry out your orders."

"I tell you, Henry, if anything'll work, this will."

"I hope so," Henry said dubiously.

"Look," Calhoon said. "What did you give me one third of Rancho Bravo for?"

"Because you saved Elias. And because we needed a fighting man—" Henry's face split in a wry grin. "Okay, Loosh. You're right. Win, lose, or draw, this is your responsibility. And we'll do exactly like you say. I only hope I git a chance at Isaacs."

"I hope you don't. Not before I do. Keep your head up, Henry." Then Calhoon galloped on.

But as he rode away from the herd, his face turned hard and sober. It was a long chance he was taking, and he could not be sure within himself whether he was taking it for Rancho Bravo or for Lucius Calhoon. All he knew was that he wanted to hurt Joshua Weymouth again. *Hurt the father bad enough and the son will have to come . . .*

In the distance the smoke seemed to double in volume. That did not surprise Calhoon; men out there were setting backfires. Shortly, with any luck the conflagration would, for the time being, be checked.

Circling the snorty herd, he rode behind the great pens where more wild cattle were imprisoned. Finding shade from the heat of the sinking sun, he took a moment to roll a cigarette and savor its smoke. For all his brave front he knew this was a last-ditch, desperate gamble and that no matter how things fell out, if Isaacs came tonight, good men would die. Maybe himself, maybe Henry or Elias Whitton. Still, there was no help for that. At least the battle, if there was one, would be on grounds of his own choosing, on his own terms.

In his mind he reviewed it all as he'd outlined it to Henry and Elias the night before and as he had set the plan up in operation.

He remembered how, as they squatted around the fire, he had gestured to another one in the distance. "Look, there're two troopers over there who'll have to go back to Double Oaks by daybreak. You think Weymouth won't question 'em?"

"Of course he will," Whitton said.

"All right. What we want him to find out is that we're doin' just fine. Actually, we're bringing' in maybe sixty head a day. But those men don't know how many. Before they leave, we make sure they know we're rounding up a hundred and that we aim to double that."

"Double it how?" Henry Gannon stared.

"All these damned thickets. Why can't they be burned to chase the longhorns out?"

Henry's jaw dropped. "Why, hell, Loosh, a man don't burn his own range."

"Whose range?"

After a moment Gannon said, "Oh."

"Burn the thickets," Calhoon said harshly. "Drive the cattle out into the open. What've you got to lose?"

Elias, comprehending, said excitedly, "We got nothin'. Weymouth got a lot. It be his land, his cattle, in sixty days."

"Right. Let him think we're not gonna leave him anything but ashes if he don't move fast. He'll be mad as a wet hen anyhow when those two bushwhackers don't show up with the receipts they were supposed to take off my corpse. Let's provoke him, provoke the hell out of him, and make him charge. We feed those Yankees tall tales about how many head we're raking in, we send up smoke enough so he knows we're in earnest about burning off the range, he'll have to come. That is, send Isaacs."

"But the herd— It'll go."

"And we'll have sixty days undisturbed in which to get it back." Calhoon grinned. "A cow boss like you can do it, can't he, Henry?"

Gannon tipped back his hat and scratched his head. "Well, we can try."

"My mother used to say," Calhoon told him, "that angels can do no better."

And now as he ground out the cigarette butt against his boot and tossed it away, Elias Whitton's answer rang in his ears. "Angels ain't exactly what's called for at this point."

Calhoon's eyes tracked the moon. Ten o'clock, he guessed, maybe a little past. The *brasada* was flooded with silver light, and its vast wildness and beauty was breathtaking. But there was no time to admire it. If they were coming, it could be any time now. He turned restlessly. From this rise of ground he could see a good distance back along the well-beaten trail from Gannon's home ranch to the South Springs Pens. They were Kansas-Missouri men, ignorant of the brush, and they would follow the line of least resistance. Confident in their own strength and in their tactics, likely they would approach the herd by this route.

Calhoon took out the Navy Colt, spun its cylinder; the brass caps winked in the moonlight. If this works, he thought, Weymouth is bound to be hurt enough . . . Gordon will have to come . . . He felt almost guilty. Henry and Elias both assumed he was fighting for Rancho Bravo, for their dream, but to him Rancho Bravo was still only bait, his bait to bring Gordon Weymouth back within his reach . . . He sheathed the gun. Then he stiffened, swung up on the Morgan, turned it to watch the trail, cocked his head, and listened.

Maybe it was only the wind blowing through the brush.

As always, just before going into battle, his stomach clenched, his mouth was dry. But the tension would be relieved with action.

No. No, it was not wind. That was the sound of many hoofbeats drumming.

Calhoon grinned coldly and, with heart pounding, swung up into the Morgan's saddle. They were coming. Now . . . now, if only no one fired prematurely, blew the trap . . .

Holding the horse tight-gathered in the brush, he looked up the moon-washed trail. Then he saw them, a dark blot strung out in double, triple file, reaching far back into the night: thirty, forty men . . . The beating of his heart leveled out with satisfaction. So Isaacs was bringing his entire force. That was good.

Now they were nearer, not knowing that in the brush on either side men were gathered, waiting tensely, giving them time to pour down there into the open on the flats. If Whitton and if Webb Peters only held to discipline . . . Whitton he was not worried about. Peters, a former lieutenant in the Confederate cavalry, was staunch, too, and authoritative. Maybe . . .

Now he could see them clearly in the moonlight. See Isaacs riding at the head, in the lead, with the man named Ed Bodie flanking him, that long, snakelike neck twisting. Isaacs had a Henry rifle in his hand, pillowed on his saddle horn. The wind ruffled his ginger beard. He rode a tall, black gelding that moved smartly, smoothly at a gallop.

Like a centaur in the saddle he was the picture of utter confidence, and suddenly Calhoon wondered if he had been right in risking this head-on clash. He had taken Isaacs twice, yes, but this man was a fighter, born and bred in a hard school, and defeat only hardened his resolve. Calhoon knew that no regular outfit was any tougher than the Kansas-Missouri bushwhackers, and Isaacs had led such a group for years. He was hard and smart, and finally he'd been unleashed, and undoubtedly he looked forward to the oncoming conflict as much as Lucius Calhoon. And those men strung out behind him were disciplined.

Then they were sweeping by along the trail, riders in the night, not bothering with flankers, confident of their strength. They passed between Calhoon's two guard contingents and headed downhill toward the prairie. Calhoon swung the Morgan, waited. He saw the rearguard go by, riding hard to keep up. Then suddenly, in the van of Isaacs' column, the night exploded with gunfire.

Calhoon threw back his head and screamed.

Above the roar of guns the Rebel yell rang out, high and shrill and ululating: the ancient cry of the foxhunter to his hounds, the awesome cry of the charging Southern fighting man. It was the signal along with the crash of weapons, and suddenly, from out of the shinnery two groups of riders burst, not along the trail, but sweeping down into the clearing on the flanks of Isaacs' Regulators.

Calhoon hit the Morgan with the spurs.

Out on the prairie the herd came to life. There was sudden bawling, blatting. Then came a rumble that jarred the very earth as the herd went into motion. More than a thousand cattle ran, and the sound of their running was enough to chill the marrow. Isaacs had succeeded; he had stampeded the Rancho Bravo herd.

And had ridden into a trap.

With the Morgan pounding under him, Loosh Calhoon raised the Henry rifle. As he came down the trail, he could see the prairie below in bold relief, high moonlight. There was the running herd, breaking north; there was Isaacs' column sweeping into the open: there was Whitton coming from one flank, Peters from another, and Gannon and his men, letting the herd go, coming from the front. More men poured in from the prairie's far rim, all hatless.

And now the night roared with gunfire, and the darkness brightened with flames, and powdersmoke swirled in the moonlight. The thunder of running cattle, their loud bawling, and that of the imprisoned, frightened stock in the pens, added to the uproar. Isaacs saw that he was encircled; as Calhoon's Morgan pounded into the opening, Isaacs' horse reared, came down. The bushwhacker's voice roared above the turmoil: "A goddamn trap! Spread out, spread out!" Then he was bent low over his horse's neck, and Calhoon lost sight of him for a moment, as the Morgan swooped into the fight and Calhoon, reins in his teeth, worked the lever of the Henry, its barrel balanced across his right forearm, its stock clamped under his left arm.

In the moonlight his targets stood out clearly: any man wearing a hat. One whirled toward him, Colt in hand, horse rearing, lining up the pistol. Calhoon raised his right arm, fired the Henry point blank. It missed the man, struck the horse. The animal went down, its rider spilling free. Calhoon clamped the gun beneath his armpit, worked the lever with his left hand, jerked the barrel around with his right wrist. As the man gained his feet and raised his Colt again, Calhoon fired once more and watched the shot spill him back.

Now, all around him guns were going off, muzzle flames bright against the dark, the smell of black powder rank, the drifting smoke a great fog. Shapes moved through it like creatures in a nightmare, seeking targets, firing when they found them. The herd, bellowing furiously, raced on at full speed, crashing now into the thickets, smashing down full-grown trees in its fright.

Calhoon crouched low over his horse's neck beneath a sleet of lead pumped by both sides, firing the Henry at any target appearing before him. Now the Regulators were completely surrounded by the Rancho Bravo men, and it was close quarters—in the war it would have been time for sabers. Horses reared and plunged, and men fired at each other almost point blank, and Calhoon threw the empty Henry away with no time to sheathe it and drew the Colt. A bearded face appeared out of the powdersmoke fog, a high-crowned hat atop it. Calhoon thrust his pistol almost squarely into it and pulled the trigger, and the face vanished in a wash of red. The riderless horse hit Calhoon's mount on the shoulder as it raced past and nearly knocked it down.

Calhoon, ears deafened, head ringing with gunfire, fought the Morgan to a standstill, searched the foggy murk of battle for one man, one horse. Then he saw it; the big black gelding, its rider hunkered behind its neck, gun in either hand, firing as he went. Calhoon swung the Morgan in the same direction, then saw a gunbarrel pointed at him. He pulled the trigger of the Colt nearly blindly, and if there was a shot, it missed him. He did not see whether he killed the man or not.

His spurs gouged the Morgan, sent it racing through the smoke cloud in the same direction Isaacs had taken. Then he was out of the swirl of cattle, pounding across the moonlit flat. As he emerged from smoke, he saw Isaacs, bent low on the black gelding, pounding toward the trail down which he'd come, in full flight, heading back to Double Oaks.

There was a bare chance of cutting him off. Calhoon swung the Morgan, gouged it with the spurs again. The gallant little horse stretched itself, giving all it had to intersect the course of the big, hot-blooded gelding. Isaacs heard the hoofbeats, swung around to look, saw Calhoon pounding across his front. His face contorted; flame blossomed from his pistol as he snapped a shot at the man bearing down on him. Calhoon heard the slap of lead close by his ear; Isaacs fired again immediately, and he missed once more. He pointed the gun again, still at full gallop and pulled the trigger, and nothing happened. He hurled the empty pistol from him with a savage gesture and brought another over. Calhoon lined the Navy Colt and fired.

He missed Isaacs. But he hit the horse, and the black gelding dropped suddenly to its knees. Isaacs went sailing over its neck, landed hard, his pistol bounding out of reach. He lay still for a second as Calhoon galloped up; then he jumped to his feet, eyes blinking rapidly, and whirled. Calhoon pulled up the Morgan, towered over Isaacs, brought down the Colt, lined it as Isaacs grabbed instinctively for his sheath knife, and pulled the trigger.

Nothing happened; either a cap had slipped or the gun was empty. Isaacs, reprieved from death, had the knife out now and made a lunge for the Morgan's belly.

Calhoon, seeing that, jerked the horse around, rearing. By the time it came down, he had kicked his feet loose from the saddle, landed like a cat in the grass. Coming up, he snapped the Colt again with another dry click; then he threw it at Isaacs, who was charging him with a foot-long Bowie. Isaacs caught it on a forearm, knocked it aside, and came in. Calhoon rolled to the right as the blade passed under his arm, and his left hand shot down and yanked the double-edged Arkansas toothpick from his boot. Then he was up and balanced and had the blade out in front of him.

Full moonglow, nearly as bright as day, shone down as Isaacs, without pause, came in, teeth bared and blade up, turning catlike after his missed stroke. Calhoon barely got his own blade up in time, and steel rang and chimed on steel as he warded Isaacs' stroke. Then Isaacs danced back. He held the Bowie out, blade parallel to the earth. He fell into a crouch, chin tucked in and back, shoulders forward, belly shielded by his left arm; the stance of the knife-fighter who knew his business.

"All right, you son of a bitch," he rasped, "you want cold steel, you'll git your share." Then he flashed in, right hand like a striking snake, blade a flickering gleam in the moonlight. For a man of his size and bulk, he was feather light on his feet. Calhoon's gut clenched. Himself an amateur, he knew he was up against a professional; he had never killed a man with a knife; Isaacs had.

He backed away as Isaacs bore in, slashing, jabbing. Once or twice he parried, but he had no opening to get in beneath Isaacs' guard. Isaacs' yellow teeth were visible in his beard as he pressed home the assault. "You goddamn Rebel bastard, I'll open up your belly—" He feinted, Calhoon responded, Isaacs thrust in hard. Calhoon tried to parry with his blade, missed, and felt Isaacs' knife slice his leather jacket. He jumped back and felt the cool swoop of razor-sharp steel slice skin on his flank. He got farther back, away from Isaacs, and the man turned, laughing.

"You ought not to carry a goddamn knife if you don't know how to use it!" Isaacs came in again, and the blade went straight for Calhoon's belly.

But this time Calhoon did not try to parry. Instead, he brought the stump of his right wrist around, and Isaacs' blade sank point-on into its buckshot-loaded end. Steel grated against lead as Isaacs leaned in with all his weight for what he thought was the kill, but Calhoon felt nothing except pressure. And now he had his opening, and his left hand came around, hard, and he felt the steel of his blade rasp against Isaacs' ribs as it entered the man's torso.

Isaacs straightened up. "Jesus Christ," he said; and Calhoon, with the knife in him to the hilt, turned it.

Then he pulled it loose. Isaacs stepped back, shirtfront turned scarlet. His face worked. "Oh, my God," he said, and his hand dropped. Calhoon moved in again, wary, but Isaacs was already in shock from the deep blow; he did not even raise his Bowie. Calhoon's blade went into Isaac's left breast, all the way to the guard. Isaacs looked full into Calhoon's face for one inexpressible second.

Then he died.

Calhoon saw the light leave his eyes. He saw Isaacs die while still on his feet. Heavily the body pitched down as Calhoon jerked the knife free.

Behind him, the thunder of combat crackled and faded like a receding storm. He stood there, dropping blade and right wrist alike, buckshot trickling from the slashed leather binding in a soft, raining patter.

Then Calhoon dropped to his knees, throat full of bile, rammed the knife into the ground to cleanse it. Over and over he chopped it in and, when it was clean, thrust it into the sheath and got to his feet and turned.

Out there on the moonlit plain it was over. Dark blotches lay on the close-cropped grass; riderless horses ran free, men spurring after them to take them up. Those riders wore no hats. In the distance there was still the receding rumble of many cattle running.

Then a voice rose above that sound: Henry Gannon's. "Come on, you bastards! The herd's gone—after it!" A horse reared, teetered in silhouette against the moonlight for a moment, came down, and vanished into blackness of brush. More riders followed it.

Still, horseless, Calhoon just stood there over the only man he had ever killed with a knife, absorbing the reaction of the fight. Then he saw a shape galloping toward him. He tensed, then relaxed as a voice, Whitton's, called out: "Loosh! You okay?"

"I'm all right," Calhoon called back.

Whitton slowed up his mount, walked it to Calhoon. His eyes gleamed in the silver light. "Oh, man," he grasped. "Oh, man, that like a buff'ler hunt all by itself. They run, we flanked 'em, bottled 'em up, and chopped 'em down. Loosh, it all work, it all work jest like you say!" Then he broke off, staring at the body on the grass. The bellowing of the longhorns in the pen was very loud. "Who that?"

"Isaacs," Calhoon said.

"Isaacs? He dead?"

"He's dead."

"Praise be. Then it over."

"For a little while," Calhoon said, and as Elias kicked free a stirrup, he swung up behind the man and rode with him to find another horse.

Chapter 10

Hollow eyed and swaying in their saddles with weariness, the three of them rode down the dusty street of Double Oaks: Calhoon, Elias Whitton, and Henry Gannon. Despite fatigue they had their rifles across their pommels, and their heads moved watchfully from side to side. Henry's left sleeve was cut off above the elbow and a dirty bandage covered a flesh wound received in the battle. He was far from being the only casualty on their side; they had lost three men in that wild, chaotic night of combat. They had lost more than that, too, with the herd scattered again in the brush. Out there on Gannon's range men, just as exhausted, were scouring the chaparral to bring in as many as possible. So there was no triumph in any of them at that moment.

Then Calhoon said, "Here. This is it." They swung their horses across the street to the little house occupied by Captain Philip Killraine and his sister, and stiffly they dismounted. As they did so, Calhoon winced; his flank was bandaged beneath his shirt where Isaacs' knife had raked it. Another couple of inches and it would have been him lying dead out there, gutted, instead of Isaacs . . . Henry and Elias trailed him as he went up the walk and knocked on the door.

After a moment it swung open. Evelyn Killraine's eyes lit at the sight of Calhoon; then her expression changed to concern and shock. "Loosh! What in the world—?"

"I'll tell you in a minute. Phil here?"

"I'm here, Loosh," the voice of Killraine said, and he emerged from another room in shirtsleeves, uniform pants, boots. He stopped short. "What the devil?"

Calhoon entered, and the other two followed. "We

123

fought Isaacs last night," Calhoon said, voice shaking a little with weariness. "He hit our herd with everything he had, but we were waiting, and we just about wiped him out."

"Wiped— Isaacs. Is he dead?"

Calhoon nodded.

Philip Killraine's face was grim. "Evelyn, you'd better put some coffee on. Loosh, Gannon, Whitton . . . sit down. Tell me about this in detail."

Calhoon told him. As he was finishing, Henry Gannon cut in. "The thing was, Killraine, that Isaacs figured that we'd have every man guarding the herd and that when it ran, we'd take after it. Only, Loosh out-thought him. We kept a light guard on the herd, laid a trap, and when the herd broke, instead of chasin' it we let it go and turned and fought. That took Isaacs by surprise and we— Anyhow, there's bodies scattered from hell to breakfast out there, and we got some wounded, too, ours and theirs. Oh, some of 'em got away in the brush, maybe a third, but mostly the Regulators are finished." He rubbed his face. "Now we got to know what to do to git in the clear. We don't want murder charges on us when all we was doin' was defendin' our lives and property."

Elias Whitton said, "We figgered maybe you could help us. We left everything jest the way it was, so if you wanta ride out and look—"

"It's like a battlefield," Calhoon added. "If it had been one or two men, maybe we could have hidden 'em in the brush but—"

"No, you did exactly right," Killraine said. Thoughtfully he drummed his fingers on the table. "So the Regulators are broken . . . and you have some wounded, some captives. Men in shape to be questioned?"

Calhoon nodded.

In addition to coffee Evelyn had cooked an enormous breakfast, which now she put before them. "Phil, you've got to do something. Especially after what we talked about last night."

"Oh," Killraine said, "I intend to do something, all

right. Exactly what, I'm not yet sure. But when you've eaten, gentlemen, we'll go have a little conference with Judge Joshua Weymouth—who, I expect, is as nervous right now as a poker player with three aces when two are already showing on the board."

Calhoon grinned, then pitched into the food. The coffee had revived him now and so had Killraine's reception. The groggy aftermath of battle was slowly being replaced with a deep satisfaction. *Hurt the father bad enough and the son will come* . . . Well, last night they had dealt Joshua Weymouth the ultimate wound. And surely now, soon . . .

With Captain Daniel Potter flanking him, Joshua Weymouth leaned back in the chair behind his desk in the county courthouse, a slight paleness of face the only sign of any discomfiture. "I don't believe any of this," he said harshly. "It's all a cock-and-bull story. It sounds to me like law-abiding American citizens were wantonly attacked by revengeful ex-Confederates. And I assure you that if that was the case, those responsible are going to pay." He looked at Captain Potter. "Right, Captain?"

"Absolutely," Potter said sternly. "And you should be the first to agree, Captain Killraine."

"Oh, I do, I absolutely agree," Killraine said. "I want the attackers punished and the rights of American citizens protected. Mr. Whitton is an American citizen, for instance. So are three other black men who hold registered brands and had cattle in that herd. Of course, the facts of the matter seem to be these—we'll have to verify them by inspection on the ground, of course. But Isaacs and his men did come on Henry Gannon's land, where they had no right to be. They did stampede his cattle and those belonging to others. And, to be sure, there are survivors to be questioned."

Weymouth slowly sat up straight. "Survivors?"

"Some of the Regulators wounded in the fight and taken prisoner." Killraine looked at Elias Whitton. "Mr. Whitton's going to swear out warrants against them for cattle rustling and attempted murder. Naturally they'll have to be tried. They ought to be able to shed considerable light on what really happened, who sent them out there to attack that herd, who they were working for—" He smiled. "I have a cousin in Connecticut who's been anxious to visit Texas. He's a lawyer, and I'm sure he'd be glad to serve Mr. Whitton as special prosecutor to make sure all the facts were brought out. Especially about whom Isaacs was working for and who sent him out there to commit those unlawful acts. You might even know my cousin's father, Judge. Maybe met him in Washington; he's the senior senator from Connecticut."

Weymouth's head jerked around. "You're Senator Morton's nephew?"

"I don't like to trade on the connection. But, yes, he did get me my appointment to the military academy."

"I see." Weymouth chewed his cigar furiously.

"On the other hand," Killraine continued, "it would be an advantage to Mr. Whitton not to have to go to court. He and the others have a lot of work ahead of them rounding up that stampeded herd. So my idea was this, strictly for Mr. Whitton's benefit. If Captain Potter investigates and files a report clearing the Rancho Bravo men— which I'm sure the facts will support—why, the captured rustlers would be turned over to the county authorities for whatever action they want to take. Then, if you wanted to have your people prosecute 'em, Judge, you could, or you could turn them loose. Just so long as there's no backlash against Rancho Bravo for defending itself."

Potter puffed out his cheeks. "I think—"

"Be quiet," Weymouth said bluntly.

Potter's face turned red; but he subsided.

Weymouth leaned forward. "There are men dead on both sides, Killraine. And you suggest we drop the whole matter just like that?"

Killraine said smoothly, "Judge, nobody really knows who killed who out there in the dark. A lengthy court trial won't really settle anything. It would inconvenience Rancho Bravo, yes. But it would also turn over an awful lot of other rocks, I can assure you of that."

They looked at one another for a moment.

Then Weymouth let out a fluttering breath. "You may be right," he said. "Very well, Captain. We'll let Captain Potter make his investigation—"

"And I'll make one of my own and file a separate report if necessary—"

"It won't be," Weymouth said. "I'm sure that the captain will find the facts substantially as you say. Rancho Bravo will turn over the wounded Regulators to him, and we'll deal with them ourselves. And there will be no charges brought against Rancho Bravo men."

"Hot damn!" Ellis Whitton exploded.

"Be quiet, Elias," Gannon said, but he was grinning.

Killraine smiled faintly. "I think that's probably the way things should fall out, Judge. Except—there's one more condition."

Weymouth's eyes narrowed. "What's that?"

Killraine's smile widened. "I believe the county should assume the expense of the burial of Isaacs and his Regulators. I trust it will." He stood up. "Well, I believe that's that. When I've read Captain Potter's report and seen it in the mail, we'll turn the captives over to you, Judge. That is, if we thoroughly understand one another?"

Weymouth stared at him a moment, then ground the cigar furiously into an ashtray, though it was not even lit.

"We understand each other," he said thinly. "Good day, Captain Killraine."

Nobody spoke until the four men were outside the courthouse and standing by their horses. Then Elias jubilantly broke the silence. "Cap'n, I swear, you laid it in to him!" He clapped Gannon on the shoulder. "Henry, you know what this mean? Way I see it, we can finally go about our business now! We still got sixty days to gather stock, and Weymouth's fangs done been drawed!"

Gannon nodded soberly. "Let's hope it works that way. Killraine, that's twice. In the same week. I don't know how the hell we can ever repay you."

Killraine smiled without much humor. "It was my

pleasure. I don't take kindly to having politicians bump me from assignment to assignment to suit their own convenience. And as for paying me— Let's ride back to the house. Evelyn will be anxious to hear how it came out, and besides, there's something else I want to talk to you about."

Calhoon caught a significance in his voice that made him look at the captain keenly, but he only nodded. "Yeah," he said. "Let's go."

When they reached the house, Evelyn pulled open the door before Killraine could touch the knob. "Phil, Loosh, how did it go?"

"It went all right," Killraine said.

"More than all right," Calhoon said. "Phil called Weymouth's bluff every way from Sunday, backed him into a corner, and used pure blackmail on him. Killraine, I'd hate to face you at a poker table."

Her face lit, and Calhoon could not take his eyes off it. "Oh," she said, "I'm so glad. Come in now. There's more coffee."

"It might be," Killraine said, "they'd like a drink. They've had a long night. Bourbon, gentlemen?"

"I ain't tasted likker in so long I don't know whether I can handle it," Henry grinned, "but that sounds like a fine idea to me. And you can make your medicine while we're having it."

"I don't have much medicine to make." They went to the dining room table, while Evelyn brought glasses and Killraine broke out a bottle. He poured drinks all around for the men, including one for himself, then stood there looking at them. "I suppose we ought to drink a toast to the end of Isaacs and his Regulators."

"I'll buy that," Elias said, and they drank.

Calhoon felt the whiskey, the first in weeks, begin immediately to unwind him. Killraine refilled the glasses, sipped a little from his own, and sat down with them. "All right, I'll make my medicine now." He looked at Henry Gannon, and for the first time he was not the little fighting cock of a man he'd always seemed; indeed, he looked hesitant, almost shy. "Could I ask some questions about Rancho Bravo, Henry?"

"Anything you want. Shoot." Gannon was growing expansive with the liquor.

"I've heard bits and pieces of what you're up to. I think I know. But I wonder if you yourself would tell me in detail."

"Why," Henry said, "sho," and he reached for the bottle again and began to talk. Philip and Evelyn Killraine leaned forward and listened intently, the girl's eyes flicking from Gannon's face to Lucius Calhoon's. And as Henry went on, waxing eloquent as he told them of his dream, her eyes began to shine with a light that seemed to pierce straight through Calhoon. "And so there you are," Henry said. "It all hangs on the good will of the Comanches, but Elias says he can guarantee that if we follow his orders on how to behave—and we aim to, one hundred percent. So if everything works out, come this time next year, we'll have it, Killraine—thousands upon thousands of acres of prairie grass, where cattle are easy to handle and git fat quick; and capital—all the gold we need from the mines of Colorado." He drained his glass, gestured widely. "The first ranch on the high plains, Phil. The first big drive to Colorado. And after that the sky's the limit. The miners in Montana want beef, too; and if we could take up range in Wyoming— Sooner or later the Indians are gonna have to give up range land. Railroads a-buildin', people from the East will soon be spillin' out . . . Beef, Phil, beef! If we have luck and got the nerve, there's no limit to how much of it Rancho Bravo can raise and sell—"

He broke off. "Of course, maybe that's whiskey talkin'. We've still got a lot of problems to solve. Money's one of 'em. But we'll do that, too, somehow. Because, damnit, it jest seems to me that if you believe in a thing hard enough, finally you'll git it. Look where we were and how far we've come—as much thanks to you as anybody."

"No," Killraine said. "So far I've done nothing that was not my duty anyhow. You owe me no thanks. But you've

made clear what I wanted to know." He paused. "Gentlemen, it hasn't been an easy decision for me to make. But
Evelyn and I've talked about it, and we've decided this—
no matter what happens, I'm not going on to Kansas. I'm
resigning my commission in the Army, and we're going to
stay in Texas."

Henry Gannon, who had picked up the bottle, set it
down again hard, staring at Killraine. "You're leaving the
Army?"

"I've come to the conclusion there's no future in it, not
for a man like me. I've never had an assignment yet where
I didn't wind up crosswise of my superiors." He grinned
ruefully. "I guess I'm not politician enough. Anyhow, if I
stay in, I'll probably wind up the world's oldest living captain of cavalry."

"But whut about that big politician uncle of yours up
Nawth?" Elias Whitton asked.

"What I told Weymouth was the truth. But—"
Killraine's face darkened. "It's a pretty sorry man who has
to depend on his relatives for his own success. No, gentlemen, I've had my run as a cavalry officer. Now I want to
try something else."

Henry Gannon and Elias Whitton looked at one another. Both stared at Lucius Calhoon, and then they turned
toward Killraine again. And Henry Gannon was cold
sober when he said, "All right. Why don't you come in
with us on Rancho Bravo then?"

Philip Killraine looked around the table, his face red-
dening. "No," he said.

Lucius Calhoon sat up straight. "Killraine—"

The officer raised his hand. "Hear me out. I said, no. I
will not take part in Rancho Bravo—not if you're offering
it to me out of gratitude for just doing my duty."

Calhoon glanced at Evelyn, and he was surprised at how
his heart had begun to pump. To keep her here . . . But before he could speak, Killraine went on. "But— Loosh heard
me tell Weymouth the other day, Texas is the coming
state. Well, I believe that, and I believe that you're right,
too, Henry, that this state will be built on cattle. I even

think that this dream of yours is going to come true, that someday Rancho Bravo will own all the lands and all the herds you talk about and maybe even more. But I can be a part of nothing in which I can't pull my own weight."

"You already have," Lucius Calhoon said quickly.

"I told you, that was my duty. We're talking business now. I'm a Yankee, remember? Wooden nutmegs? The almighty dollar?" Killraine's grin was wry; then he sobered. "Your herd is scattered, Henry. How many extra hands would it take to get it all back together? Twelve, fifteen?"

"Lord God," Henry said, staring. "If we had that many more, Isaacs wouldn't have hurt us at all."

"Especially if they were being paid wages instead of cattle," Killraine said. "Right?"

"Right! Then every beef they branded would be for Rancho Bravo—"

"And when you had your herd together, ready to make your drive . . . I know little about such a thing. Won't you need supplies and equipment?"

"I told you," Henry said, voice excited. "Money. That's our big stumblin' block. It's what keeps me layin' awake nights. Wonderin' where I'm gonna raise the money for what we need for that drive." He shook his head. "Men can't travel all that distance just on beef. They got to have flour, coffee, some kinda dried fruit or they git scurvy. When you're trailin' two, three thousand cattle, you need a cook and some wagons to carry the gear . . . And we're desperate for more horses; we need 'em for huntin' cows, and we need 'em for the drive. Most of all, we need powder and lead and fixed ammunition for our repeaters and presents, lots of presents for the Comanches, any other Injuns we have to deal with. And the things to build a ranch house with and cold weather gear for the drive on up to Denver. There's a thousand things we need and not a dime to buy 'em with until we git to Colorado . . ."

Philip Killraine nodded and fingered his moustache. "I thought that would be the situation." He paused, then blurted: "Henry, Evelyn and I have a little money. And we've talked it over, we sat up all night talking about it.

We both want to stay in Texas, and we're both fascinated by Rancho Bravo. Would three thousand dollars buy ten percent in it?"

Henry's jaw dropped. "Three thousand dollars?" He whispered the sum in awe.

Lucius Calhoon, staring at the Killraines, felt a surge of jubilation. It was as if a key had finally fitted into a lock or a ghost had taken on solid flesh. Three thousand dollars! That was the crucial difference, the money to turn Rancho Bravo from a dream into solid, triumphant, profitable reality! He looked at Evelyn, and now his mind raced ahead, for the first time in years daring to make plans, envision a life beyond the present. And then, harshly Elias Whitton said, "No."

Calhoon and Henry whirled on him simultaneously.

"No," Elias repeated. "That money won't buy no ten percent. That kind of cash speaks for a full quarter of the outfit. You come in, Cap'n, you come in same as Loosh did, an equal partner."

"I couldn't," Killraine began. "You can't give away piece after piece of Rancho Bravo until there's nothing left for you—"

"One quarter of Rancho Bravo be plenty for any man," Elias said. "And we ain't give away something for nothing yet." He grinned. "We got this far by giving away nothing for something. Me and Henry, we started with two pieces of a dream. We fit 'em together, it a little more solid, but it still close to bein' jest a wisp of fog. We trade off some of that fog to Loosh Calhoon, and it turn into cattle. But movin' them cattle still a dream. Now we trade you the last piece of dream, and then everything turn real. So where me and Henry each started out ownin' nothing but half an idea apiece, now we own one quarter each of a real business, a real ranch. Seem to me we run our stake up purty good. From nothin' to twenty-five percent of somethin', I satisfied with that. I say there a place for you, Cap'n, and that you've mo' than earned it. It the last place open, you take it, from now on we got all we need. You mind the business; Henry, he got the final say on handlin' cows; Loosh, he the man when it come to whatever fightin' we got to do; and on the trail and among the Injuns I got the final say. So there you are, Rancho Bravo all one piece now. You wanta come in on that deal, we be proud to have you." He looked at Calhoon and at Gannon. "Any argument on that point?"

"None," Calhoon said, feeling that somehow his world, his whole life had been transformed. His eyes still on Evelyn, he felt years of bitterness and hopelessness fall away from him like an outgrown skin just shed; and in that moment he was a new man. He looked down at his maimed wrist, and for the first time since he could remember, it did not even seem to matter.

"And I say none," Henry Gannon added. "Killraine, you're in."

Evelyn burst out, with excitement, "Phil! Oh, Phil!" Eyes shining and a little moist, she turned to Elias, then to Henry, and finally to Calhoon. "Thank you. Thank you all."

Killraine's grin was wide. "Well," he said quietly, "it seems we have a deal." And he stood up and put out his hand for each of them to take.

Then he poured more whiskey and raised his glass. "Gentlemen," he said. "I give you Rancho Bravo!"

Chapter 11

Two months later Lucius Calhoon reined in his brush-scarred Morgan once more on the crest of a rise and looked at the enormous herd on the holding grounds below: four thousand longhorns, all colors of the spectrum, grazing almost placidly on the huge open prairie where circling riders kept them together, only occasionally dashing after a wild one making for the brush. They ranged from thick-necked, snuffy bulls to unsteady, blatting calves, and three-quarters of those cattle wore the Rancho Bravo iron; Calhoon shook his head in a kind of disbelief. Compared to these brush-popping Texans, he was still an amateur, and if he had not been witness to it all, he would have thought it impossible for such a herd to have been brought together in so short a time.

But Henry Gannon's cow-sense and Phil Killraine's money had accomplished it. The capital Killraine had supplied had made it possible to hire extra riders, so the cow hunt could continue while the stampeded herd was rounded up—and this last had been easier than any of them had dared hope. Partly herd broken, the cattle Isaacs had stampeded could be driven in by bunches instead of being dragged in one by one; and, of course, they were already branded. Also, the men were better fed now and stronger, with better mounts and more of them, since Killraine and Elias had combed the county for good cowhorses.

But in the long run, it was Henry Gannon's skill and effort that had put this herd together. It was almost as if Henry himself had been suckled by some wild old longhorn cow; there was no end to his knowledge of the breed or the tricks he used to catch his stock. Carefully taming and breaking a bunch of fifty, he used them over and over for bait, turning them into a thicket, leaving them for a day or two, and then when half their number of wild cattle had joined them, pushing them with comparative ease into the open. The wild ones followed, sometimes all the way to the herd.

Or he built traps at hidden springs where cattle came to drink, and every night a few riders penned several head with a minimum amount of manpower and effort. One of his weirdest stratagems was to slaughter an animal in a clearing surrounded by thickets and drench it and the ground all around with blood. That scent brought cattle from all sides to paw the carcass, gore it, and make day and night hideous with an eerie, mourning bellowing: a cow-funeral, Henry called it. Blood maddened, such animals were dangerous but unwary, and daring riders could rope them before they broke for cover.

And, of course, they had burned the brush, using wildfire to drive the cattle inward from the outlying corners of Henry's land toward the center. It was a tactic of desperation and one no rancher would use, save sparingly, on his own range. But as Calhoon had pointed out, this was no longer Henry's range; soon it would be Josh Weymouth's.

Weymouth. Calhoon's single hand tightened on the reins. Apparently he had accepted defeat. Philip and Evelyn Killraine had moved from town to Henry's home ranch once Killraine's resignation from the Army had been accepted, but Phil still kept close watch on developments in Double Oaks. "What's left of the Regulators have cleared out," he reported. "Josh has made no effort to hire any more. He was downright cordial to me the other day. I guess he knows when he's licked. Anyhow, he's getting what he's started after all the same—Henry's range. And maybe what? A thousand mavericks left on it, the outlaws Henry says are too wild to bother with anyhow, too much trouble to drive and hold. He'll have those and their increase. My guess is he figures that's enough, and it's not worth stretching his luck any farther."

Elias Whitton had not been so sure. "All the same, we got to be ready for anything. Weymouth, he remind me of an Apache. You take a Comanche or a Cheyenne, now he don't care which way the odds fall; he'll go to war jest for the hell of it and git hisself killed for the honor. But a Apache, he fights for loot, nothin' else, and he figgers a man that sticks his neck out until he got the odds with him is a damn fool. He don't hit you when you lookin' for it; he wait 'till you least expect it. For all we know, Weymouth jest waitin' for the balance to swing the other way again."

At the time Calhoon had been sure Elias was right, Killraine wrong. But all these weeks had passed, and Weymouth had made no effort to block them, indeed had paid them no attention at all. More significantly, Calhoon thought, he had not brought Gordon home.

Sitting there on the rise, looking down at the herd, Calhoon was half surprised to find himself glad of that. He rubbed his left hand thoughtfully over the leather-bound, shot-loaded stump of his right wrist. Three months ago he would not have believed anyone who had told him he would feel this way, but now— Suddenly unable to contain his eagerness any longer, he put the Morgan into a lope and galloped down to the flats below, swinging wide around the herd.

Henry Gannon was at the two wagons parked some distance from it, and laid out on the ground on tarps were every manner of goods which he and Philip Killraine and the Mexican cook were double-checking. "You sure that's going to be enough flour for all these men?" Killraine asked.

"No. But enough to git us to San Antonio, plus a little extra. We'll stock up there. Prices are cheaper, I hear," Henry said, "and anyhow, the longer we can put off buyin' stuff that'll spoil, the longer it'll keep when we git on the trail." Then he heard Calhoon come up. "Loosh," he said, "all quiet out yonder?"

"Like a Sunday School," Calhoon said, and staring at the supplies, he felt again that eagerness. "Henry, tomorrow morning?"

Gannon laughed, a jubilation in his voice that matched Calhoon's. "At daybreak, Loosh. That's when we move 'em out. Elias, he's gone to take another look at the route for the first day's drive, make sure we can keep in the clear and out of the brush all the way. Come mornin', we're gonna push this beef and push it hard, walk the legs plumb off it, so when nightfall comes, they'll all bed down like little babies. I figure by noon we'll be off my land or Weymouth's or whoever the hell's it is, and when that happens, Rancho Bravo'll really be on its way to the Pecos!" He tipped back his hat, blue eyes shining. "By God, Loosh, it's hard to believe, ain't it? But it's true!" He turned toward the herd, swept out his arms. "There she is. Every man that didn't want to go to Colorado has cut his stock out or sold off to us for a dollar a head on the hoof. Four thousand head and over thirty riders to push it on, and God help anybody white or red that tries to stop us with a crew like that!" He slapped his leather-clad thigh. "Loosh, the dream's come true! Sonofabitch, I'm so excited I can hardly stand still!"

"You're not the only one," Killraine said. "I've got a feeling in my belly, you know? Like just before a battle. Like every hour between now and the time we move will be a day. Texas! By damn, the best thing the Army ever did for me was send me here and then send Potter to replace me! If they hadn't disgusted me like that, I might have spent the rest of my life in uniform and missed this adventure completely! It's . . . it's all just so big I can hardly comprehend it!"

Calhoon grinned, then sobered. "Phil, where's Evelyn?"

"At the ranch house. She swore that Weymouth wouldn't get his hands on all that fine old furniture that belonged to Henry's mother. She found a place to store it in Double Oaks, and she's been packing all day long. It all ought to have been hauled in and put away by now, and later on, when Henry builds his new house out beyond the Pecos, he can freight it out—"

"Right," Calhoon said. "Well . . ." He reined his horse around.

"Loosh," Henry called, "where you goin'?"

Calhoon turned in the saddle, grinned back at him and

Killraine. "Since nothing can stop us now," he called, "I've got a little business at your house, Henry. If you need me, you'll find me there." And suddenly he let out a Rebel yell and spurred the Morgan, leaving Killraine and Gannon staring at one another.

It was nearly twilight when he reached the ranch house in its sheltering spread of live oaks. Reining in the Morgan, he approached it at a more sedate pace, though impatience hammered within him—impatience and a kind of fear as well, an apprehension totally unlike anything he had ever felt going into combat.

His face sobered. What he had to do, he had perhaps put off too long already. But it was something he could not have done, had no right to try, until this moment, until he was sure that Rancho Bravo could not be stopped. But in the morning that great herd would swing out into motion like a giant, restless snake, its leaders pointed west, and once that happened, the die was cast. There were risks ahead, yes, but of a different kind— And besides, Gordon Weymouth had not come back to Double Oaks.

He swung down off the Morgan, tethered it, and strode toward the house. His stride was long, steps firm, his spurs jingled as he went up the steps, but his one good hand was sweaty, and his mouth was dry. He shoved open the front door, entered a vacant living room, passed through that to the kitchen. There Evelyn Killraine, in a plain housedress, her hair falling about her face in damp, curling tendrils, packed a wooden coffee box with odds and ends. As he entered, she straightened up, turned. "Loosh!" She smiled, but her face went pink, and she automatically shoved back her hair. "I'm such a mess—"

"No," Calhoon said. "No, you look fine." Then he went straight to her, and before she could move, he put his arms around her and pulled her to him strongly, and then he kissed her.

For one astounded moment her body was rigid beneath his grasp, her lips clamped. Then, suddenly she went slack and moved against him, and her lips yielded, and she returned the kiss. Calhoon held her for a long time, and during that interval nothing else in the world mattered. Her arms were about him, every curve of her body tight against the hard, flat planes of his, and something within him soared at the knowledge that her hunger for him matched his for her.

When they finally broke apart, she stepped back, face very pink, staring at him with huge green eyes as she touched her hair again. She looked dazed. "Loosh Calhoon—"

"Evelyn Killraine," he grinned, subtly mocking her. "Only we're gonna change that. Evelyn Calhoon. How does that sound?"

She sat down suddenly on the box she had been packing, and now there was moisture in her eyes. "Loosh. Is this a . . . proposal?"

Calhoon was dead serious now, going to her, kneeling, taking her hand. "It is. I love you, Evelyn. I reckon I have from the day I woke up in that hospital tent. But there wasn't . . . I mean, there were reasons why I couldn't say anything, do anything about it until now. Until now I had no right . . ."

She stared at him. Then her face lit with a smile, and her hand tightened on his. "You had every right. I've been waiting and waiting, hoping . . . Oh, downright shameless . . . And you talk about no right . . ." She stood up, trembling a little. Then she whispered, "Oh, Loosh. Yes. And kiss me again—"

It was much later when they began to talk rationally. "Tomorrow," Calhoon said, "the herd moves. By nightfall we'll be out of this county, beyond Weymouth's reach, and Rancho Bravo will be real. That means I'm not just a bankrupt cripple any more but a man with property and a future. I had to wait until I was sure of that before I dared ask you—" His face went hard. "Sure of that and one other thing . . ."

"I don't know what you mean. You could have asked me any time . . . And your hand. Do you think that matters?"

"There was a time when it did. There's a lot you don't know about me, Evelyn."

"And a lot I do, too. Don't you think I've talked about you with Henry and Elias? Without you there wouldn't have *been* any Rancho Bravo!"

Calhoon stiffened. "But they didn't tell you how I lost my hand. They didn't tell you why I came to Texas."

"No." She looked at him wonderingly.

"Then I guess I better had," he said. "I want you to know everything before we're married, so if you want to change your mind . . ." He backed away, gathered his thoughts while he rolled, one-handed, a cigarette. Then brutally, bluntly, he told her. About Belle Isle. About Gordon Weymouth. About the punishment cell and about the surgeons . . . "And so," he said, "after I had seen what they had done to the plantation, to my home . . . It was like all of that settled on Weymouth's head, too, was part of the debt he owed me. And . . . I didn't believe in Rancho Bravo at first, you understand? Not the way Henry and Elias did. All I saw in it at first was a way of fighting Joshua and bringing Gordon home, where I could kill him."

He let out a long breath. "But he hasn't come. And now I thank God for that, because if I had killed him, I would have been a fugitive on the run, no way I could have had you. The best thing that has happened to me is that I didn't find him and that he's not come back. Now, tomorrow we leave. And then it doesn't matter any longer, you see? I'll never come back to Double Oaks, I'll never see Gordon again. And even if I do, I have too much now to . . ." He rubbed his face. "It's like I've been down in a dark pit that no light could reach, and now I've climbed out into bright mornin' . . . And it was Rancho Bravo, that and you, that pulled me out."

"Loosh," she said and came to him.

He held her. "Now I've got too much to lose. Now there's a future. And as long as there's that, Gordon Weymouth doesn't matter anymore."

"Thank heaven for that," she whispered.

"So," he said, "when we get to San Antonio, we'll be married. We'll swing south of San Antone, resupply there. That'll give us time. I'll stay with you a few days, then ride like hell to catch up with the herd. And when we've made Colorado and sold off, I'll be straight back for you."

"No," she said. "No, leave me in San Antone? And you gone months, maybe a year, and me not knowing what has happened to you?"

"It's the only way. A drive like this is no place for a woman. A thousand miles with four thousand wild cattle. Indians, not just the Comanches that Elias can deal with, but maybe southern Cheyennes or Apaches . . . No. No, when Rancho Bravo is staked out above the Big Bend country and we've sold the cattle at the mines—"

"Now wait a minute, Lucius Calhoon . . . It's not going to work like that at all." She stepped back, and her voice was sharp.

Calhoon stared at her. "You think I'm going to marry you and then have no husband for all that length of time?" she went on. "Sit quietly in San Antonio doing needle-point? You're crazy!"

Calhoon frowned. "Now, honey, don't you start—"

"I'm not starting anything," she said. "But I'm not waiting in San Antonio. You're right, you don't need me on the drive, I'd only be in the way. But there's no reason why I can't go on to Denver by stage and wait for you there, is there? Nor do I have to be a useless ornament. By the time you get there, I'll know who the best buyers are and have everything lined up for the sale of the cattle . . ."

Calhoon stared at her. "Why, you already got everything planned!"

She laughed. "Lucius Calhoon, I've been planning for longer than you'd believe. All I was afraid of was that you'd never ask!"

"Why, you little—" Then Calhoon laughed, too, and he caught her and held her to him. While he was kissing her again, hoofbeats drummed in the yard outside.

In due time she pulled loose from his embrace. "I have a feeling that's Phil, Henry, and Elias."

"Why, sure," Calhoon said. "And me, I have a feeling there's gonna be a party!"

In the gray light of false dawn the vast *brasada* was a rolling ocean of brush. If, Calhoon thought, he had been a hawk circling high overhead instead of a man, he would have looked down on a scene unbelievable in its awesomeness. The wagons and the horse herd had already moved out. Now the trail herd was forming: four thousand bunched longhorns coming to their feet off the grassy bedground with a sound like a massive sigh and a clicking of horn on horn that made a noise Calhoon had never heard before, a wild rattling. With Evelyn mounted side-saddle on a good bay horse beside him, he watched, from the rise he had sat on yesterday, the mobilization by Henry Gannon of an army of wild cattle and an army of wilder riders.

A great, varicolored blot in the dimness, the herd was shaped and molded by Gannon as a sculptor might have molded clay. In the lead were tame oxen; both were white. Behind them, point, swing, and flank riders squeezed the herd out in a long line. Drag riders brought up the rear, and horsemen galloped out and back, turning unbroken cattle trying to make one last dash for the safety of the shinnery. Behind the herd the sky was lightening; ahead in the west it remained black. Bulls bellowed, cows and steers bawled, calves blatted, shattering the morning silence with their protests.

Henry was everywhere, up and down the line, passing instructions from man to man. He handled the herd with the delicacy of a housewife handling fine, easily-broken china, all too aware of the chancy nature of the cattle, the still inherent wildness of them. Before the lead oxen Elias Whitton sat on his buckskin like something carved from ebony, watching Henry, waiting for the signal.

Evelyn let out a sigh, and Calhoon felt her hand covering his as it rested on his saddlehorn. Their horses were so close their thighs touched. "Loosh," she whispered. "They're about to start."

"Yes," Calhoon said. He glanced toward the east again. Now an orange rim of sun appeared above the brush. As its rays flashed with startling quickness over the great land and fell on the herd, there was for a moment a kind of hush as if even the cattle held their breath. Then Henry Gannon, on the right flank, stood up in his stirrups and swept off his hat and held it high.

All along the giant herd every man did the same. In the lead Elias lifted his sombrero. Henry's eyes went up and down the line. Then he dropped back in the saddle and clapped his hat back on.

Yellow and orange in the east; a new day dawning and there was a tightness in Calhoon's chest as he saw Elias Whitton clap on his own hat, then lean out of the saddle to touch the off ox with a goad. The big animal broke into a shambling walk, and its mate followed suit. As the oxen began to move, the band of tamer longhorns just behind followed automatically. Now the sun was brilliant, teetering on the horizon. In fresh morning light the herd, like a reluctant snake, began its crawl toward the west.

"There they go," Evelyn whispered, and her hand tightened on Calhoon's.

He said nothing. The emotion in him was too strong. Rancho Bravo; it was on the move, and with every step of that giant herd the past and all its strife and bitterness were left behind. Everything that had ever happened up until now was drowned in the sound made by four thousand protesting animals and sixteen thousand moving hooves. The herd was on its way.

"Oh, Loosh," Evelyn said thickly beside him. "Oh, Loosh, it's so beautiful. I'm sorry. I can't help crying."

Calhoon leaned over, put his arm around her. But he did not take his eyes off the herd. There was a burning in his own eyes; and an almost uncontainable feeling of strength and masculinity in his loins. What was down there moving west was not just a herd; it was the future of the state of Texas, maybe of the whole western frontier. The country he had fought to rip apart had come together again, and maybe someday the wounds would heal. Out there lay a whole new world, as large again as the one that had just locked itself in war and bitterness. Out there was where you began again with everything in the past forgotten. Anyhow, the men who filled that unknown country would need the beef. When Evelyn straightened up, he said, a little hoarsely, "Let's ride down and follow."

All that day men worked like demons in a swirl of dust, pushing the herd on inexorably at exactly the speed Henry Gannon had calculated it would take without breaking up or trying to stampede. At the same time the men fought desperately to contain the bunch quitters who wanted to turn and head for their own home thickets. Horses neighed and hooves pounded and loops whirled and cattle bawled; and yet somehow, Henry Gannon managed to hold it all together, that great, tenuous, fragile chain of cattle. He exhausted three horses, four, but he was always on the go.

Calhoon, Philip Killraine, and Evelyn, inexperienced at working stock like this, stayed well ahead of the herd and tried not to get in the way, knowing that, for the time being at least, each of them might do more harm than good. Sometimes Killraine rode with Elias, who kept his post ahead of or alongside the white lead oxen. Evelyn and Calhoon rode together, content in the company of each other and the excitement of the drive.

There was no nooning nor would there be any on this drive. Lucius Calhoon and Evelyn pulled aside at noon and ate beef jerky and cold biscuits and washed the meal down with water and watched the herd move past, like a great, swaying army, and then rode out ahead again. By one o'clock they had swept off of Henry Gannon's land— only it was not his land anymore; today was the deadline, and already the notice of auction for back taxes would be posted at the courthouse. Realizing that, Calhoon thought about Henry's statement last night, as Gannon had restlessly prowled the house empty of its furnishings.

"I was born here, growed up here," Henry had said. "It kinda hurts to leave. But it feels good, too. My old man come out here from Tennessee. His before him come to Tennessee from eastern North Car'lina. The Gannons always move west once a generation, seems like . . ."

Elias, who had marked out the route, kept them on open prairie, well away from the thickets. Yet, as if the herd were a magnet, wild cattle came from far away to join it, mavericks, unbranded. By late afternoon they had picked up maybe a couple of hundred head.

And by then the cattle were handling easier, tired from the day's long march, half a dozen troublemakers roped out and killed. They were becoming an entity, as if each longhorn were a cell of a single great body. Well out in front Calhoon and Evelyn were joined by a jubilant Phil Killraine. Then near sundown Elias Whitton and Henry Gannon loped up.

Henry was weary, but he was too drunk on triumph to pay attention to it. Ahead lay vast reaches of open prairie with a line of trees marching across it, marking the course of a waterway. "Yonder's Boston Creek," he said. "That's the county line. We'll ford tonight—nothing to it, it ain't hock deep—and bed down on the other side. Once we're past that timber, we're out of Weymouth's territory. Tomorrow mornin' when we wake up and start to drive, we can fergit Josh Weymouth and concentrate on handling cattle." He shook his head. "I'll swear," he said, "being clear of Weymouth's like havin' a tooth stop achin' . . ."

"Yeah," Calhoon said; and he thought of Gordon. The man seemed hardly now to exist. "Yeah, you're right. Exactly. Henry, we've—" And then he broke off as, above the thirsty bawling of the cattle, a new sound sliced the air.

Evelyn said something incoherent, wondering, but every man there knew that sound well.

It was the loud blare of a bugle.

"Son of a—" Henry Gannon grated and reined his horse around.

Then they saw them, galloping down the line of trees, the blue-clad troopers riding straight up on their horses, the troop guidon flying in the van, the fat captain, Potter, bouncing in his saddle as they came. Flanking him rode two civilians, and Harry Gannon growled something deep in his chest. "Speak of the goddamn devil," he said. "Josh Weymouth."

But Calhoon had no eyes for that man. He was looking at the rider on Potter's other flank; tall, wide shouldered, brawny, and no older than himself. The man sat on his mount with confidence. As the cavalry crossed their front and Potter bellowed a command and the troop swung into line and cantered forward to meet them, Lucius Calhoon's left hand dropped to the butt of his holstered Colt, and all the old ferocity welled up in him unhampered.

The man riding on the captain's right, his wolfish face split in a grin, a pistol on either hip, was Gordon Weymouth.

Chapter 12

"Company—halt!"

Captain Daniel Potter reined in abruptly, steadying himself with his left hand on the pommel of his McClellan saddle, raising his right in the signal. Behind him the line of cavalry, forty troopers, spread out in front of the creek, facing the on-coming herd, pulled up. On Potter's flanks Joshua and Gordon Weymouth checked their horses.

Gannon said thickly, "Phil, what—?"

"I don't know," Killraine said. "Elias, you'd better turn back and stop the herd."

"Stop it, hell!" Henry snapped.

Killraine whirled on him. "Check it, anyhow, until we see—" He gestured. "Those are *my* men out there. United States soldiers!"

Calhoon said, not taking his eyes off of Gordon Weymouth, "Elias. Go stop the herd."

Whitton grunted something, spun his horse. Then Potter and the Weymouths were trotting forward.

"Come on, Henry, Loosh," Killraine said hoarsely. "Let's see what they want. Evelyn, you wait here." He spurred his mount, and the others rode with him. Calhoon, as he approached the trio flanked by two noncoms with leveled carbines, felt a sense of unreality. *No,* he thought. *No. Not now, just when—*

But the man on Potter's right was no ghost from the past conjured up by longing; he was solid, tangible, Calhoon's size and heavier, a lean, well-joined, though lanky duplicate of his father with the same tapering features that Joshua Weymouth had and which had haunted Calhoon in countless dreams. The only difference was that now Gordon had a small moustache.

149

And as the three riders approached, he raked eyes like two small jet beads across them and slowly smiled. "Killraine," he said. "Gannon. And . . . Calhoon."

Calhoon sucked in breath. "So you remember me."

Gordon Weymouth was dressed in brush clothes like Calhoon's own. He leaned forward, pillowing arms on his saddle horn. "Of course I remember you. I always remember stubborn cases." He smiled, and it was like the snarl of a coyote, the way his lips peeled back from sharp teeth. "How are you, Captain? No wiser, it appears."

"No," Calhoon said.

Then hoofbeats drummed, and Evelyn rode up beside him, put a hand on his arm. "Loosh . . ."

"Get back," Calhoon said harshly. "That's Gordon Weymouth."

"I know," she said and reined her horse closer to his. He knew what she was doing. He could not start anything with her like that in the line of fire.

Then Killraine said, "Potter, does this maneuver have any special point and if so, what?"

Potter mopped his sweating face with his sleeve. "I'll let Judge Weymouth speak to that. But you are not to cross that creek and leave the county, and if you try, my men will drive you back. You're not to leave Judge Weymouth's jurisdiction."

Calhoon and Gordon Weymouth were looking at one another, and Calhoon hardly heard as Gordon's grin grew more mocking and Gordon's eyes ranged with unabashed interest over Evelyn. Calhoon's right hand, which no longer existed, seemed to hurt intensely, almost unbearably. It was with effort that he wrenched himself away to hear Joshua Weymouth speak.

"Ahh, Gannon," Weymouth said heavily and in an officious voice. "And you, Philip Killraine, and Lucius Calhoon and all others with any vested interest in the enterprise known as Rancho Bravo and built on the basis of the Gannon herd, former brand J—Bar—G and earmark overbit on right, undercrop on left. Be it known to you here and now, by order of myself, Joshua Weymouth, as district agent for the Treasury of the United States, that all cattle in this trailherd branded with the mark Rancho Bravo are hereby impounded as contraband, namely property of the government of the Confederate States of America." He cleared his throat. "Said Confederate contraband to be appropriated for the use and benefit of the United States, later to be disposed of at auction." He turned. "Captain Potter, you will have your men impound that herd of cattle."

"Yes, sir," Porter said. And after that there was a moment of absolute, dead silence.

Then Henry Gannon spurred his horse forward. "Confederate contraband? Weymouth, what the hell is this?"

Joshua Weymouth grinned slowly. "Why, Gannon," he said, "it was a close thing, and if Gordon hadn't ridden God knows how many horses to death between Washington and here, maybe you'd be across that creek and beyond my jurisdiction. But I knew they had to be there somewhere."

"They had to be— What?"

"Mr. Gannon," Potter cut in. "Take your hand off that gun. I warn you, sir, if there is any hostile action, my men will open fire immediately."

Henry hurled an obscenity at him, then turned back to Weymouth. "You'd better start explaining—and fast."

"I think I'll let Gordon do that," Weymouth said easily. "After all, he's the one who unearthed the documents and brought them here. Gordon?"

For the first time the younger Weymouth took his eyes off Calhoon, swung to confront Henry Gannon. He fished inside his brush jacket, brought out folded papers. "I knew they must be there," he said, in a nasal voice. "And they were, in the recently captured records of the Confederate government and especially the Army of the West, all of which were sent to Washington. I had to spend a lot of days going through papers, Gannon—"

"Make sense!" Gannon snapped. "What're you talkin' about?"

"Why, letters," Gordon said easily. "Letters from your father, Joseph Gannon, to General Kirby Smith. The first one dated November 20, 1864, offering to make all the cattle bearing Joseph Gannon's brand or on his range available to the Confederate Army in the West without charge. And when no answer was received, another one dated January 4, 1865, renewing the offer . . ."

Gannon sat up straight in his saddle. "Daddy died in February of '65—"

Gordon Weymouth shrugged. "It makes no difference. To all intents and purposes he turned his entire herd over to the Confederate Army. That makes the herd property of the Confederate Army as of November, '64. Every cow that Joseph Gannon owned. And the increase thereof. All Confederate property, horn and hoof. And therefore subject now to expropriation by the Treasury Department, Joshua Weymouth, local agent, and impounded now in the name of the United States Government by the US Army for later sale at auction. In other words, Gannon, you don't own that herd. Your daddy gave it away to the Confederate government, and it's Confederate property taken over by the United States. So all those cattle out there—" he gestured widely "—don't belong to you and never have since 1864."

For a moment there was no sound save for the bawling of cattle checked short of water. Then Killraine urged his horse forward. "Mr. Weymouth, may I see those letters?"

"You may not," Gordon said and returned them to his pocket. "But you can look at the order my father signed if you want to."

"I demand to see those letters." Killraine shook his head impatiently. "They don't mean a thing unless you have an official acceptance from the Confederate government. That's a matter of law; I know, I've been involved in this sort of thing before."

"Sure it's a matter of law. If you want to take it to court, you can see the papers then." Gordon sat straight in his saddle, and now his eyes and face were hard. "All that concerns you right now, though, is a duly issued writ of attachment issued by Joshua Weymouth, federal Treasury agent, for the Rancho Bravo herd as former property of the Confederate Government. That writ—" he jerked his head "—is now in possession of Captain Potter, who will proceed to execute it."

Killraine swung toward the officer. "Potter, I warn you, you're involved in an illegality. Maybe you've justification if there's an acceptance from the Confederate government of Mr. Gannon's offer. Otherwise, sir, you're on damned treacherous ground."

Potter's doughy face flushed. "Killraine, you know the general orders of this detachment as well as I. My concern's not with the legality of Judge Weymouth's writ, only with the fact that he's issued one. It's up to my command to enforce that writ and to impound and take possession of the property it covers. I intend to have my men do that and by force of arms if necessary. The writ, incidentally, covers only those cattle in which Mr. Gannon has an interest. Owners of other brands are free to cut their stock out of your herd and proceed to whatever destination they have in mind. But all the Rancho Bravo cattle will be returned to the range from which they came and held there until disposition by public sale or otherwise. You, of course, have recourse to the courts. But right now, if you interfere with my men, you'll have to take up arms against soldiers of your own government."

"Well, by damn—" Henry began.

"Hush," Killraine said sharply. Then he said, "Potter, we've got to confer. Give us a few minutes." He wheeled his horse. "Henry, Loosh, Elias— Come on."

Gannon and Elias turned their horses. Calhoon only sat his, looking at Gordon Weymouth, Evelyn crowding her mount close by his side. "Gordon," Calhoon said softly. "I came here looking for you, you know that."

"Well, now you've found me," Weymouth said, smiling. Then his smile went away. "You raised stink enough in that prison, Calhoon, so that they sent me west to a rotten post on the Missouri. I thought about you out there, and you know what? I only wish I'd tied the ropes tighter on that left hand so it would have come off, too. But maybe this is just as good."

Calhoon drew in a long breath, and Rancho Bravo was

forgotten, everything was forgotten except Weymouth's grinning face, shimmering through a kind of red haze that obscured Calhoon's vision. Then Evelyn gripped his arm, nails biting deep. "Loosh—" At the same time Killraine roared, "Calhoon! Come on!"

A measure of sanity then returned to Lucius Calhoon. "We'll see," he said thinly, and then he pulled the Morgan around and, with Evelyn galloping by his side, face pale with relief, rode to join the others.

He swung down where Killraine, Whitton, and Henry Gannon squatted in council. Killraine's face was pale. "Henry, could your father really have written such letters?"

Freckles were blotches on Gannon's rough-hewn features. "I don't know. Hell, yes, I reckon he could have. He loved the Confederacy so much he woulda give the clothes he wore to it, stripped himself buck naked for it. Yeah. Yeah, likely he wrote the goddamn things."

Killraine let out a gusty breath. "Then we're done for."

"I'll be damned!" Gannon flared. "All we got to do is stampede that herd, run it right across that creek, plumb through them soldiers! I'd like to see those bluebellies try to stop four thousand hellbent longhorns!"

Killraine stood up, and his voice crackled. "You attempt that, and by God, I might shoot you myself! I'll fight Weymouth, but not my own army!"

Gannon jumped to his feet. "Why, you damned Yankee, I oughta knowed—" In his fury his hand swooped down, and that was when Elias grabbed him from behind, pinning his arms against his torso.

"Henry," the black man snarled, "don't you touch that gun!"

For an instant Gannon appeared about to struggle; then he eased. "All right," he said in a calmer voice. "You can let go, 'Lias. Phil, I'm sorry—"

"Skip it," Killraine said. "I don't blame you. But what we've got to face up to now is reality. If we try to fight the army, we're all outlaws, and Rancho Bravo's finished anyhow. Besides, we can't ask the riders to do such a thing; Weymouth's let their cattle go and the ones who've hired on for wages . . . Can you expect them to do it for fifteen, twenty a month? No. This is a matter to be settled in the courts." He paused. "The thing about it is, those letters in themselves don't justify Weymouth's action. He has to have some record of the Confederate government accepting your father's offer and taking title to the herd. If he doesn't, he can't make his case stand up. My hunch is that he doesn't, or he'd have bragged about it, waved it in your face. But the only way we'll find out is in court."

"Court," said Calhoon bitterly. "And how long will that take and how much money?"

Killraine looked down at his boots. "A long time," he admitted. "As long as Josh Weymouth can make it last. And as much as he can make it cost. Of course, meanwhile, he'll take title to your range and hold the herd there. If the government wins, he'll collect impoundment fees from it for grazing the herd—"

"And if we win?" Calhoon asked.

"He'll charge us the same."

"And when we can't pay those, it'll start all over gain," Calhoon said bitterly. "I've seen it happen in South Carolina; that's how they took my cotton. They know you haven't got the money to fight it in court, and it's their court anyhow and—" He clenched his left fist, slapped it against his leggings. "What you're saying, Phil, is that one way or another Rancho Bravo's finished."

"I refuse to admit that," Killraine said.

"We've got some money left," Evelyn put in from where she sat on her horse. "And we've got a house in Hartford we can sell. And don't forget, we've got an uncle who's a senator—"

"That's not it," Henry said bitterly. "It's time, don't you understand? If we're delayed, somebody else will get a herd through to Colorado, skim off the cream of the market. Meanwhile, Weymouth'll let the cattle run wild, and they'll have to be dug out of the brush one by one again and—" He shook his head. "We've just got time to make Denver with the herd before snow comes anyhow; if we lose a season, we've lost everything . . ." He turned away, head down, so they could not see the working of his face.

"No. No, he's won, damn him. Even if we win in court after six months or a year, he's whipped us." The words seemed torn from his very entrails. "Rancho Bravo's finished."

For a very long moment no one spoke, watching Henry. Apart from them he stood with head down. Presently he turned, and when he did, his face was set, he was in control once more.

"But we'll make him work for it," he said quietly. "I want to see a bunch of horse soldiers tryin' to drive these *ladinos* back to their old range. And, by God, Phil, if you'll put up the money and use whatever influence you got with your uncle, we'll do our best to fight it down and make that herd cost him, anyhow." He tried to grin and failed. "It's your baby now, Killraine. This is the kind of fighting you'll have to lead. Me, I've gone as far as I can go."

"All right," Killraine said. "We'll fight—but in the courts. Now, we'd better go talk to the men. Explain to them our drive is stopped, but they can cut their cattle out and go on, if they want to. I don't see how they can, though, without supplies or Elias to guide 'em. I imagine Weymouth'll make 'em a rock-bottom offer, and they'll sell out to him." He turned to Calhoon. "And— Loosh."

"Yeah."

"You stay away from Gordon Weymouth." Killraine's eyes were hard and narrow. "I'll not have any explosion that'll ruin what little chance we have left."

Calhoon did not answer. He felt as if everything inside him were frozen, as if nothing that were human in him worked any longer.

"Loosh," Elias said, almost pleadingly. "Ride with us. You a better talker than us. Talk with the men, explain . . ."

"Explain," Calhoon said harshly. He swung up in the saddle. "Explain what? That it's over, finished, that they can sell their little bunches to Josh Weymouth for fifty cents a head if they want to, or maybe a quarter?" His voice rose. "Tell them that it's all gone, blown away like dust in a hot wind—"

"Loosh," Evelyn said. "Please, darling—"

He looked down at his wrist. Then he lifted rein. "All right, Elias. I'll ride with you and tell the men."

They had fought Yankees before, of course, and they wanted to fight them now. There were seven or eight of them left with cattle in the herd, maybe a hundred or a hundred and fifty head each. They had fought thorns and spikes and wicked horns and half-broken horses and gunmen to gain title to those animals, had been prepared to trail them a thousand miles, fight Indians, too, or whatever or whoever came against them because, at the end of that drive there was Colorado gold, and gold meant independence, a fresh start in life, hope. Now they were told that all their dreams were false, that they were balked even before they had begun. They could not drive on without supplies or Whitton to guide them. They could not turn back because they owned no range on which to graze their stock. Like Rancho Bravo, they were now wholly at Josh Weymouth's mercy, and most of them were, in their fury and bitterness, for charging head on with the herd through the cavalry. It would take more than forty horse soldiers to hold four thousand cattle when they broke. All of Calhoon's persuasiveness was required to convince them not to do that, and even as he managed to calm them, he hated the sound of his own voice, its tinny hypocrisy, its oily promise. He was telling them that there still was hope when he himself knew that all hope was gone.

"Courts," the man named Webb Peters said and spat. "Yankee courts. How far you think you gonna git in them, Calhoon?"

"I don't know," Calhoon said. "We don't know anything yet."

Peters looked at him directly and almost with contempt. "Well," he said, "we'll hold the herd tonight all in one bunch. We can't cut stock this late anyhow. Tomorrow—" He spat. "God knows what we'll do tomorrow."

"I can ask no more than that," Calhoon said. "I wouldn't even if I could." And he whirled the Morgan and galloped back toward the herd's point, Henry and Elias following.

Killraine and Evelyn met him there. The soldiers were spreading out now, encircling the herd. A detail was putting up a tent for Captain Potter. "Well?" Killraine asked tensely.

"I talked them out of fighting. Tonight anyhow," Calhoon said harshly. His eyes swept the open prairie. "Where're the Weymouths?"

"They rode back to Double Oaks," Killraine told him. "Said they'd have enough riders here in the morning to take over the herd and push it back to Henry's—Weymouth's—range."

"I see," Calhoon rasped.

Then Evelyn spurred her horse forward. "Loosh—"

"Yeah?"

Her face was grave. "Ride with me. For a little while."

He nodded. "Yes. We have things to talk about."

In silence they galloped their horses toward a grove of mesquite near the creek, and there Evelyn reined in. "Loosh," she said, eyes enormous, pleading, and she put her hand on his. "You've got to understand. It doesn't change anything—not between us."

Calhoon took his hand from under hers. "It changes a lot."

Evelyn sat straight in the saddle, face pale. "How could it?"

"How could it?" He laughed bleakly. "I told you, I didn't dare ask you, had no right to ask you, to marry me until Rancho Bravo was more than a crazy dream. Well, I thought for a little while— I thought a lot of things for a little while. I should have known better. The wild blabbering of a fool Texan, an ignorant nigger and . . . a bankrupt cripple . . . crazy. All of it crazy."

"Loosh, don't talk like that. I've never seen you like this before. We haven't lost yet, there's still the courts—"

"Yeah, the courts." He laughed again, still with that cold sound, still feeling completely frozen within himself. "So you and Phil can go broke like the rest of us, waiting for justice. No." His voice rang out bitterly. "No, Rancho Bravo's finished, and you'd better see that now, Evelyn. Everything's finished. The only thing left is—" He raised his wrist. "Well, anyhow, I did what I set out to do. I hurt the father bad enough so the son had to come. Only now I wish—"

"Loosh—"

"Skip it," he said brutally. "Forget it, Evelyn. Write it off, you hear? All of it. Just like Rancho Bravo. It was all a dream." Then, before she could speak again, he wheeled the Morgan and rode away.

"Loosh!" she screamed behind him, but he neither turned nor answered. He rode toward the parked wagons as fast as the Morgan could stretch itself, and there he pulled up short, as Killraine, Elias, and Henry stared at him.

He paid no attention to them. He went to the tailgate of the wagon, pulled a notebook from his pocket, found a stub of pencil, wrote rapidly in bold strokes, signed it with a flourish. Then he ripped out the sheet and, leading the Morgan, strode around the wagon, and thrust the paper at Philip Killraine. "Here," he said, in a voice like steel on steel. "Anybody who wants to can witness my signature on that."

Killraine looked at him blankly. "What—?"

"The paper," Calhoon snapped. "Take it. It returns my interest in Rancho Bravo to the three of you, to be divided equally. I'm out of it now, you see?"

Henry Gannon's jaw dropped. "Loosh, you gone crazy?"

"No," Calhoon said. "I've gone sane. I should have known all along that nothing counted except what I came to Texas for. Anyhow, I was under false colors, Henry." His mouth curled coldly. "I was just using you. Just using Rancho Bravo. All I wanted was to bring Gordon Weymouth back, and now I've done that. So I'll go about my business. The business that brought me here in the first place."

Whitton's eyes were wide; then they narrowed. "Calhoon, you ain't gonna—" He took a step forward.

Then he halted. Lucius Calhoon's left hand merely seemed to twitch, but suddenly it held the Colt Navy, cocked, and lined. "Stand back, nigger," he said harshly.

"You don't stop me. Nobody stops me. I'll shoot the man who tries, you hear? Or the man who follows me. The three of you, you're in the clear. Stay that way."

"Loosh, you can't—" Gannon said.

"I told you, stay back." Calhoon menaced them with the pistol, even as he stepped backward to the Morgan's flank. Then, in one quick, lithe move he had wrapped his right arm around the horn, found the stirrup, was in the saddle. Gun pointing down, he looked from one of them to the other. Evelyn was whipping her mount, galloping toward the wagons. He had to hurry; he could not face her again.

"Nice knowing you," he said ironically. "If you ever get across the Pecos, maybe I'll drop in sometime. That's where I'll be heading if I leave Double Oaks alive." Then he whirled the horse and spurred it savagely and was gone.

Chapter 13

Once, riding hard, he looked back.

Only one rider tried to follow him from the wagon: Evelyn. Calhoon cursed and turned the Morgan toward a distant thicket. When he looked back again, she had checked her mount. A lonely figure on the flat in the dying light, she sat there motionless, bent over, face in her hands.

Calhoon swung forward, left hand in a fist. That was, of course, an additional debt to settle with Gordon Weymouth.

For the moment he felt no grief. Indeed, he felt nothing at all, and that suited him just fine. For a while he had been afraid that Rancho Bravo and Evelyn Killraine had made him human again. But if they had, it had not lasted long. He was once more what he had been when he had come to Texas, a machine with a gun, designed for two functions only: hating and killing the object of his hating. Whatever humanity had been left in him had been scooped out today, and he was empty of everything save determination.

With no pursuit he dodged the thicket's edge, stayed in the open, though he reined down the Morgan to save the animal. There was no reason why it too should pay Gordon Weymouth's debts.

Even shoved as hard as they could push it, the herd had covered less ground in a day than a lone rider could traverse in a quarter of that time. The last light had died, but the moon had not yet risen when, ahead, Calhoon saw the scanty yellow spangle that was Double Oaks in the darkness at the bottom of its bowl. He pulled up the Morgan and let it blow. He himself felt no fatigue despite the grueling day: only impatience and a cold satisfaction that, after all this time, it must soon be over. Sometimes he seemed to hear Evelyn's voice or see her face, but always he managed to blank that out with another memory: of himself hanging by ropes in the punishment cell, mad with thirst. That was enough to blank out anything.

When the Morgan was rested, he put it down the hill. He was, he judged coolly, a little early. The chances would be better if he waited another hour, maybe two, for the town to simmer down and go to bed. He had a little money in his pocket; not much, only two hundred percent more than he had come here with before—two dollars. That would buy a drink or so, but not in a downtown saloon. He did not want the Weymouths to know he was here.

But there was a *cantina* in the outlying Mexican quarter, small, dirt floored, with bugs circling the rank betty lamps of rancid tallow that lit it. Its few patrons and its owner stared at the gaunt, one-handed Anglo who, hitching his mount to a donkey pen behind the place, strode in, asked for *mescal,* paid with silver, and took a table in a murky corner, his back to the wall, to nurse the drink.

It was strong and brutal liquor, and Calhoon sipped it gingerly, not needing it to give him courage or bolster his resolve and maybe a little afraid that alcohol would bring emotion back. He wanted no emotion; he wanted no memory of Evelyn to intrude and weaken his resolve. He made the drink last a half hour and felt nothing from it, ordered another, and nursed it for the same length of time.

The second one touched him but only a little. One day, he thought; one lousy day and then they would have been beyond Josh Weymouth's reach. If only Gordon had not found the letters until a day later, or if only one of the horses he had ridden in relays had gone lame; if only Isaacs had not scattered the herd and it had started earlier . . . If only . . . There were so many ifs. None counted, so it must have been meant to be like this all along.

Most of the Mexicans had left the cantina. One sat

slumped drunkenly at a table, head on his arms, dreaming God knows what in the misery of utter poverty. Calhoon thought: *Now it is time.* The man behind the bar stared at him as he took out the Colt revolver and carefully checked its caps and loads and then restored it to its holster.

Calhoon stood up. After all, he thought, Evelyn would find another man. One whole, two handed, with money and property, and sane, not always drunk with the need for vengeance. In a sense Gordon Weymouth had done her a favor.

That thought did not help at all. He put it away from him and left the bar, mounted the Morgan in the darkness out back, and turned onto the broad, single street of the town.

Up ahead a few saloons were still open; but there was almost no traffic, either on foot or horseback. Closer at hand the residential section was nearly totally dark. Only in a big frame house a few hundred yards away did lights burn behind curtained windows; and Calhoon knew whose house that was. He rode past it on the far side of the street, in shadow, head down, like a tired or drunken man bound for home. But covertly he searched the shadows around it with his eyes. He did not think that tonight the Weymouths would leave themselves unguarded.

He was right: a Union soldier lounged on the house's porch; another paced wearily back and forth in the side yard; likely there would be one more behind, another on the house's other flank. It would not be a simple matter to get to Gordon Weymouth tonight.

Calhoon kept the Morgan walking. At least, he amended the thought, for a man who cared whether he lived or died. And there he had the advantage.

He reached the street's end, halted under the shadows of the plaza's trees. There he rolled and lit a cigarette; and while he smoked it, he thought. After a while he had what he was going to do worked out, and he tossed away the butt and rode the horse back down the street.

As he went, he took the single gauntlet that he wore in the brush from his belt, reversed it, and pulled it down over the stump of his right arm. Only the fingers were left empty, and they were stiff enough to stand by themselves.

The light still burned in the house. The soldier beside the front door puffed a cigar, his rifle grounded. Sure enough, another trooper patrolled the other flank, so the house would be surrounded. Calhoon grinned wolfishly. As long as he could get in, it made no difference. To someone who cared whether or not he got out again, it might have.

He rode up to the gate of the picket fence enclosing Weymouth's property, swung down, and ground-reined the Morgan. He opened the gate and strode boldly up the walk, and as the soldier saw him coming, he jerked erect, bringing up his gun. Calhoon raised his hands—or what appeared to be a pair of them—over his head.

"Don't shoot," he said. "The judge sent for me."

"Maybe," the soldier said. "Keep those hands high."

"Sure," Calhoon said and came up the steps. Disregarding the gun, he went boldly to the door, arms still lifted. The soldier stepped aside to cover him, and in that instant Calhoon swung the shot-loaded right wrist.

The man had no chance to dodge. With terrific force the leather bag of shot slammed against his head, and he sighed and crumpled, and Calhoon caught him before his body could thud to the floor. Quickly he laid the soldier out, tossed his rifle off the porch and into the yard, and then, heart thudding, everything within him no longer frozen but feeling as if it were all aflame, he tried the front door. It was unlocked, opening easily. Calhoon drew his Colt, stepped through it, found himself in an entry hall with no one in sight. He closed the door soundlessly; to his left there was a living room, also empty. He stepped into it.

Weymouth lived well; the furniture in here was good; there was a piano and the face of a weak-chinned but pleasant-looking woman stared down at Calhoon from a crayon portrait on the wall. Weymouth's wife, Calhoon supposed, knowing that she had died long before. Weymouth, Gannon said, had loved her well. It seemed strange to think of Weymouth as capable of loving anyone. But, Calhoon thought with satisfaction, if he loved Gordon, so much the better.

Beyond the living room there was a dining room and, after that, Calhoon supposed, a kitchen. There was no light in the dining room, and he edged into it. Sure enough, as he crouched in darkness, he saw an oblong of light beyond. At an oil-cloth covered table, Joshua and Gordon Weymouth sat with a bottle between them, Gordon's back to Calhoon. Calhoon held his breath for a moment in the shelter of a huge old sideboard and listened.

"I tell you," Gordon said, "I hired four clerks, and we looked for it everywhere. They never sent him any answer. If they had of, I'da found it."

"Well, it's not absolutely vital," Joshua said. "Old Joe's letters were at least enough to act on. But it's tricky, you know? Cotton, the courts assume it's Confederate contraband because the Confederate government controlled its sale. But beef's another matter. All the same, I can string it out until they're busted."

He arose, went to the curtained window, stood there broadside to Calhoon, hands in hip pockets, shoulders hunched like some sort of roosting bird of prey, lamplight glinting on his iron-gray mane.

"Busted," he said harshly. "That's the main thing, to bust Henry Gannon like his daddy busted us. Your mother, God rest her soul— I'm convinced she'd be alive today if it wasn't for Joe Gannon."

"Well, she can rest easy in her grave," Gordon said. "Come tomorrow mornin', it's all paid back."

"Yes." Weymouth's voice was quiet. "I hope she knows that. And I hope she knows how much you did to bring that about." He turned. "Son, it's so damned good to have you back. I was so damned lonesome—" He came around to Gordon, put his hand on the younger man's shoulder. Both their backs now were toward Calhoon, and he eased out of darkness. "You know," Weymouth went on, "most of this is for your sake anyhow. A man likes to leave his son something—"

Calhoon, stepping out into the open and, lining his gun, said quietly, "Josh. Gordon. Don't either of you move.

This is Lucius Calhoon, and if you move or holler, I'll kill you both."

Three, perhaps five, seconds passed while both Weymouths sat frozen. Then Gordon, not turning, said hoarsely: "Calhoon, how'd you get in?"

"You supplied me with the means."

Josh Weymouth's voice shook a little. "Calhoon, you can't get away with this. All I have to do is call the guards—"

"If you do," Calhoon said, "you'll both be dead before they can come through that door. Now, Gordon, on your feet, real slow and easy. Josh, you stand well aside."

The elder Weymouth moved a couple of steps to the right. Gordon tensely shoved back his chair and arose. Strapped to his right hip he wore a Navy Colt. There was, on his father, no sign of a weapon.

Calhoon said, "Take off that pistol, Gordon. Very carefully. And throw it across the room."

Gordon Weymouth did not move. "You aim to shoot me in cold blood?"

"You just take that gun off. There was—" Calhoon's voice was not steady "—a time when you had me strung up like a goddamn pig at hog-killing time. And you laughed at me and asked me how I liked it. I told you something then, remember?"

"I don't—" Weymouth began.

"I told you that you couldn't run far enough or dig deep enough to hide from me when I got loose. I meant it. The gun, Gordon." Calhoon moved up closer.

Slowly Gordon Weymouth's hands moved. The belt came loose.

"Across the room."

Gordon threw it. It landed in the corner with a solid *clunk!*

"Now, turn around, both of you."

They did, perfect targets in the brightly lighted room, Calhoon in the darkness, vague. Josh Weymouth's face was soft and slack with fear, and Gordon's mouth twitched as he looked at the gun.

"All right," he whispered. "I'm slick, Calhoon. But if you pull that trigger, you're dead. The guards will have you before you ever leave this place."

"That," Calhoon said, "is my worry." He lined the Colt on Gordon Weymouth's left breast, and his finger tightened on the trigger. He waited for Weymouth to cry out, beg, move, do something to make him punch the shot. But before he could pull the trigger, Joshua Weymouth sprang, throwing himself between his son and the muzzle of the gun, hurling himself straight at Calhoon.

It was a wild, crazy, gallant thing to do, and Calhoon stepped aside a single stride and swung the gun in a choppy arc. Weymouth grunted as the barrel struck his skull a glancing blow and lurched on by, dropping dazedly to his knees, then falling on his elbows.

"Hold it!" Calhoon snarled as, in the same instant, Gordon Weymouth turned toward the gun he'd flung away. Gordon froze, and as he raised his hands and swung toward Calhoon again, his eyes shuttled to his stricken father and then to the muzzle of the Colt and all color drained from his face, leaving it the white of paper.

"Calhoon—" The word was a husky whisper. "Please, please don't—"

Calhoon stared at him. The right hand that no longer existed hurt with excruciating pain, and all he had to do was pull the trigger and it was over, all over. But that was not enough. Not enough to pay for the hand, not enough to pay for Rancho Bravo, not enough to pay for Evelyn Killraine. Suddenly a wild cry burst from Calhoon's throat, a mad, strangled sound. He let down the hammer of the gun and threw it across the room to join Gordon's Colt. Then he raised his good left hand and his right wrist. "Now, God damn your soul!" he whispered.

Gordon blinked. "What—?"

"Come at me. Come at me, you bastard, if you've got the nerve!"

Then Gordon Weymouth understood, and suddenly the fear left his face, color returned, and he grinned. "With hands? Why, you must be mad!"

"Yes, I'm that," said Calhoon. "Come on."

When Gordon laughed, there was confidence in the sound. "Oh, for God's sake, I've got two and you—" Then his face twisted savagely. "You Rebel bastard, I'll kill you!" He rushed at Calhoon.

Calhoon swung the right wrist. It smashed into Gordon's face, and Gordon grunted and reeled back. Under the impact of the pound of shot he shook his head dazedly. "I don't—" He tried to right himself, but Calhoon was already moving in. This time he swept the wrist back from the left; Gordon tried to raise an arm, but the loaded leather hit his cheek and laid it open, and he rocked across the room. He slammed against the stove and reeled off against the wall, and Calhoon went after him. As Gordon tried to regain his balance, Calhoon chopped the wrist down into his face. Gordon's nose went, smashed beneath the heavy lead and leather, and his chin and chest turned scarlet. He shook his head, tried to raise his hands, and Calhoon chopped at the right eye. His wrist hit full; blood poured from brow and cheek, and Gordon howled. Calhoon hit him again on the other eye, and Gordon dropped to his knees. Calhoon bent and seized his shirt front with his left hand. As he jerked Gordon erect, motion caught his eye. Josh Weymouth, on his feet, hurled himself across the kitchen, scooped up Calhoon's gun from the corner.

Panting, he whirled, bringing the Colt into line. Calhoon, in one swift motion, jerked Gordon to his feet, swung him around, sapped and blackjacked and dead weight; and Josh Weymouth, yelling something incoherent, stood paralyzed with the pistol aimed at his own son's body.

Gordon's head lolled as Calhoon held him high. "Calhoon," he managed. "In the name of God—"

Still holding him as a shield, Calhoon smashed him in the mouth, felt teeth give beneath the blow and knew a savage satisfaction. Gordon was still alive, but one more blow, two—

"Guards!" Josh Weymouth screamed. "Guards, help, murder!" And he pointed the Colt straight up and fired off three rounds in one long blast, and the back door immediately smashed open.

Calhoon hardly heard it. He was no longer in this kitchen in Double Oaks; he was in a sweltering cell, whole body ablaze with pain, right hand's stink rank in his nostrils, the stench of his own dead, rotten flesh. He was biting on a wooden plug while the saw rasped on bone and he made a thin screaming sound; he was staring at a burned plantation house; looking into the eyes of Evelyn Killraine as she saw her future, her dreams, crumbling. He raised his right arm for a final blow, and his muscles felt not like flesh but like parts of a mighty, destructive engine, ready to drive home irresistibly. And then Elias Whitton's voice sliced through his madness as he yelled, "Weymouth! Drop it!"

Calhoon swung his head, Gordon's dead weight dragging in his hand, the loaded right wrist cocked. He stared uncomprehendingly at the back door, at Henry Gannon and Elias Whitton standing in it, guns drawn and aimed at Joshua Weymouth. Weymouth's jaw sagged. "You. You two—"

"Thass right," Elias said. "Us two." He made a pantherish stride, rammed his gun into Weymouth's belly, reached up, and took the Colt Weymouth held poised, and jerked it free of Weymouth's grasp.

Calhoon found words. "Henry. Elias—"

Suddenly Josh Weymouth was crying, his voice full of pleading. "Gannon, Whitton, for God's sake, you got to stop him! *He's killing my son!*"

"I can't help that," Henry Gannon said coldly. "He's come a long way to do it."

"No, no, you don't understand, don't let him kill Gordon—" Weymouth's voice was a high, bubbling whine now. "Don't let him do it, Gordon's all I got—"

"It's not our affair," Henry said. "We just come to make sure Calhoon was safe."

"But, you don't— Listen! Listen, please, I'll trade you, I'll trade you Rancho Bravo for Gordon! Don't let him kill him, I'll give you an order to Potter, release your herd I never had . . . there wasn't proper proof nohow. Only, don't let him hit Gordon again with that goddamned thing!"

"That's up to Calhoon," Henry Gannon said.

"No, shoot him, do you hear? Shoot him before he kills Gordon! Do that, I'll give you Rancho Bravo back! Shoot him, Gannon, if you want your herd!"

"Go to hell," Gannon said bitterly. Then he said, "Loosh—"

Calhoon stared at him through red-swirling eyes, loaded wrist still cocked.

"Loosh," Henry said, "he wants to make a trade. Rancho Bravo for Gordon Weymouth. But it's up to you, Loosh. Either way. You can choose. We won't interfere."

The mist seemed to clear a little. "What?"

"It's your personal affair. Didn't you hear Josh? You got to choose. Rancho Bravo—or Gordon."

"Choose," Calhoon repeated.

"Shoot him!" Josh Weymouth begged. "If you want your cattle, shoot him!"

"Shut up!" Whitton said fiercely. "You think we'd shoot Loosh for *you?*" He turned to face Calhoon. "Loosh, you go ahead and do whatever you think you got to do. We done took out all them guards, and we ride you out safe if you kill that man."

Calhoon closed his eyes, opened them again, looked down into that bloody mask, then understood it all; and with his leather-bound wrist still high, knowing that one more blow would do what he had dreamed of for so long, he let Gordon Weymouth drop.

Gordon fell at Calhoon's feet on knees and elbows, making a mewing, whimpering sound, the floor beneath his face puddling quickly with red. Calhoon put out a boot, pushed. Gordon rolled limply over on his back. Calhoon looked down into the red smear that had been a human face.

"All right," he said hoarsely. "The face is gone. Fair trade for the hand."

"Jesus," Gannon said, staring at Gordon Weymouth's countenance.

"Oh, Gordon—" Josh Weymouth moaned and started forward. Calhoon blocked him, caught his shirt, jerked him upright. "Listen," he rasped. "I heard you and Gordon talking. You never had a case against Rancho Bravo.

So you write that order, you hear? You write it, and you write it now, good and clear and definite, so Potter can't question it. Or otherwise this ain't over. Otherwise, I will come back, and what I did to Gordon just now will only be the beginning."

Joshua Weymouth's face was like tallow; his tall, gaunt body was trembling. "Do you think I want you back?" he whispered. "After the way you've mutilated my son? I wish I'd never heard of you, Calhoon, all I want is to . . . to see you gone. Let me go. I'll write it now. Then . . . will you let me see to Gordon?"

"I'll see to him," Whitton said. "Where's some water and a rag? You go ahead and write."

"By the sink," Weymouth said, voice quavering. "Into the living room, Gannon. Where I've got pens and paper."

"We'll want those letters," Henry said. "The ones Gordon brought from Washington."

"I'll give them to you. I'll give you anything. Only, for God's sake, take that mad man and go."

They went out. In the kitchen Elias crouched over Gordon with a damp cloth, mopping at his face. He looked up at Calhoon with a kind of awe. "You didn't leave much."

"Good," Calhoon said. "I don't want a day of his life to pass that he don't remember me. Every time he looks into a mirror, I want him to remember the day he strung me up and the fun he got out of it."

"He will," said Elias. "Never fear, he will." Then he began to mop away the scarlet.

Chapter 14

The eastern sky was streaked with dawn as the three men trotted their horses toward where the herd lay bedded. Between Henry Gannon and Elias Whitton, Lucius Calhoon swayed in the saddle with fatigue. He felt strangely drained and empty; now he had nothing left—neither his hatred for Gordon Weymouth nor his love for Evelyn Killraine. After his treatment of her last night that must be as smashed as Gordon Weymouth's face. He clung to the saddle with his single good hand on the horn and only wished he could share the jubilation of Henry Gannon and Elias Whitton.

"It warn't no trouble to take all three of them guards out," Elias laughed. "Any good Comanche coulda done it without blinkin'. But it jest plain luck we got there when we did. One more punch and Gordon Weymouth and Rancho Bravo both gone!"

"No luck to it," Henry Gannon said in a quieter voice. "The choice was up to Loosh. It had to be. Me, maybe if I'd been in his boots, I'd have thrown that punch. Regardless of what it cost."

"Shut up," Lucius Calhoon said fiercely. "Be quiet, both of you. You damned fools. Why didn't you stay away?"

"Because you one of us," Elias Whitton said. "You part of Rancho Bravo, win, lose, draw, or any paper you sign. You think we let you ride in there and git your fool self killed all alone? Everything gone anyhow. We come in to make sure that if you git Gordon Weymouth, nobody else git you."

"You damned fools," Calhoon said again harshly.

"Maybe," Henry said. "But then, if we weren't, there wouldn't have been no Rancho Bravo anyhow. But if you want to kill him, Loosh, if you still feel like you got to do it, we'll go back and help you, anyhow. No matter what it costs."

"Shut up," Calhoon snapped again. "I don't want to kill him. Gordon Weymouth and I are even."

"Okay," Henry said. "Simmer down. Anyhow, we tore up that paper you give us, even before we rode in." Then he drew rein. "Look yonder," he said in a different voice.

The others checked their horses. They were on a rise, and below them in the first light of morning, the herd still slept, circled by riders, some in civilian clothes, some in blues. Beyond there was a row of tents. Closer at hand the wagons with their white tarps stood out against the green.

"Ain't that a sight?" Henry said thickly. "Look at them. Look at all them cattle ready to line out. Ain't that a sight?"

Lucius Calhoon kept the Morgan tight-reined. "It's a sight," he said in a voice he could not keep quite steady.

"Let's go down easy," Gannon said. "We'll tell Phil, and then we'll all go to Potter. As soon as the soldiers are withdrawn, we'll explain to the men." Then he turned to Calhoon. "You don't have to be part of that, Loosh. We'll handle it."

Calhoon whirled on him. "What do you mean, I don't have to be—"

"I think you got some more urgent business," Henry said. "Look-a-there. She must have sat up all night waitin'."

Calhoon swung around. Then he saw the rider leave the wagon, gallop across the flat toward them, sitting on the horse strangely, not astride but side saddle. Something leaped within Calhoon. Once more he felt as if he were out of the dark pit into the bright light of day. "Evelyn," he whispered.

"We tried to explain why you felt like you had to do what you did. Sometimes those things ain't easy for a woman to understand. You'll have some talking to do, I guess—" Henry broke off. Calhoon heard his laugh swept away by the morning wind as he touched spurs to the Morgan and raced down across the flat to meet her.

As it turned out, there was no talking. Evelyn only reined in her horse so hard it reared as she cried, "Loosh, thank God you're back and safe!" And Calhoon swept the Morgan up alongside and put out his handless right arm and wrapped it around her and lifted her from the saddle and held her against him for a moment, then lowered her, and dropped off his horse himself. He stared into her face, pale skin, red mouth, enormous eyes, and then as he reached for her, she moved into his arms.

Captain Potter examined the papers dubiously. "I don't understand this," he said. "I don't understand it at all. But . . . it looks official."

"It's official," Philip Killraine said. "There's the seal."

"Yes." Potter rubbed his jowls. "Yes, that's true, it is. 'All claims public and private against the Rancho Bravo herd voided.' And Josh Weymouth's signature and seal. Still, it's very strange."

Killraine took the paper from his hands. "Be that as it may, Captain, there it is, take it or leave it. You have two choices. Either remove your men or fight to stop that herd. Because, in twenty minutes, on this authority we move it out."

Potter rubbed his face again. Then he said, "Captain Killraine, you would not resist the United States Army if this paper were not valid."

"No," Killraine said. "You know me well enough to understand that."

"Then," Potter said, "I shall recall my men. Only . . . Captain, you've been here longer than I have. Are affairs in Texas always this complicated?"

"Captain," Killraine said, "after a spell you'll find that Texas is a complicated state. Good day, sir." And he then turned and left Potter's tent.

With his horse crowded close to Evelyn's, Calhoon watched now as the horse soldiers drew away from the herd. It had been allowed to water along the creek, and it was a great, rainbow-colored blotch against the green as riders formed it up. Morning light glinted on thousands of horns. Across the flat the blue-clad ranks of cavalry were drawn up and watching curiously. Calhoon saw Henry place the two white oxen, saw the riders, point, swing, flank, and drag, take their places all along the line.

Once more, like master sculptors, they molded the great herd into shape. The air was full of the sound of bawling cattle and blatting calves. Down there by the two white oxen Elias Whitton waited.

"Loosh—" Evelyn said, and her hand closed on his, but neither took their eyes from the herd.

Calhoon's gaze followed the figure of Henry Gannon, mounted on a *bayo coyote* mustang, galloping down the length of the herd. Henry swung around the drag, came up the near side. He stopped to talk to riders, his fresh mount curveting, held in check by a strong hand. Then he swung the horse around, rode off some distance from the great, spread-out herd.

Calhoon watched, breathless as Henry stood up in his stirrups, swept off his hat, and raised it high.

Down there at the herd every rider duplicated the signal to show that he was ready.

Henry Gannon clamped the sombrero back on. Elias Whitton dropped into his saddle, fixed his own hat in place, and touched an ox with a goad. The animal lurched into motion. Its mate moved out, too, and then behind it the other cattle began to walk. The morning silence rumbled with the sound as four thousand longhorns lurched into motion, heading west. Across the prairie, a bugle blew, and the blue-clad ranks of cavalry strung out into a column in the opposite direction.

"There they go," Calhoon said, helpless against the life, the eagerness, and the hope that stirred within him at the sight. "Bound across the Pecos."

"Yes," said Evelyn, and when he looked at her, she was smiling, and her eyes were glowing. Then she touched her mount with her whip. "We mustn't be left behind."

"No," Calhoon said and spurred the Morgan and galloped after her as the lead oxen crossed the shallow creek, climbed the other bank, and behind them the great herd followed, pointed toward an unknown land.